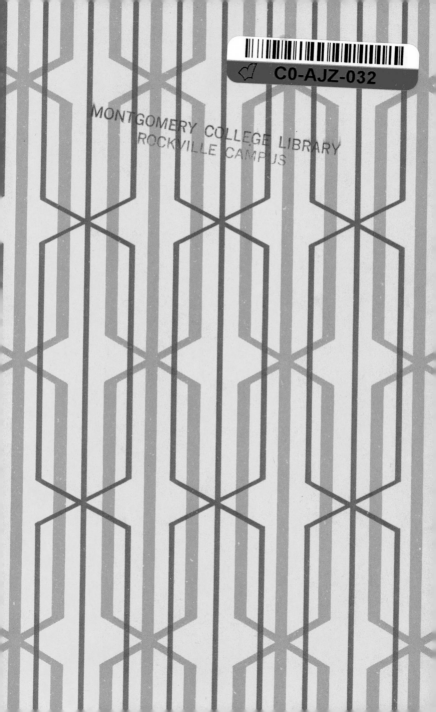

Noughts and Crosses.

Noughts and Crosses

Stories Studies and Sketches

by
SIR ARTHUR THOMAS QUILLER-COUCH
(Q, pseud.)

" Ipsae te, Tityre, pinus,
Ipsi te fontes, ipsa haec arbusta vocabant."

Short Story Index Reprint Series

BOOKS FOR LIBRARIES PRESS
FREEPORT, NEW YORK

First Published 1888

Reprinted 1969

STANDARD BOOK NUMBER:
8369-3269-2

LIBRARY OF CONGRESS CATALOG CARD NUMBER:
77-103527

PRINTED IN THE UNITED STATES OF AMERICA

TO MY WIFE.

CONTENTS.

NOUGHTS AND CROSSES.

THE OMNIBUS.

IT was not so much a day as a burning, fiery furnace. The roar of London's traffic reverberated under a sky of coppery blue; the pavements threw out waves of heat, thickened with the reek of restaurants and perfumery shops; and dust became cinders, and the wearing of flesh a weariness. Streams of sweat ran from the bellies of 'bus-horses when they halted. Men went up and down with unbuttoned waistcoats, turned into drinking-bars, and were no sooner inside than they longed to be out again, and baking in an ampler oven. Other men, who had given up drinking because of the expense, hung about the fountains in Trafalgar Square and listened to the splash of running water. It was the time when London is supposed to be

B

empty; and when those who remain in town feel there is not room for a soul more.

We were eleven inside the omnibus when it pulled up at Charing Cross, so that legally there was room for just one more. I had travelled enough in omnibuses to know my fellow-passengers by heart—a governess with some sheets of music in her satchel; a minor actress going to rehearsal; a woman carrying her incurable complaint for the hundredth time to the hospital; three middle-aged city clerks; a couple of reporters with weak eyes and low collars; an old loose-cheeked woman exhaling patchouli; a bald-headed man with hairy hands, a violent breast-pin, and the indescribable air of a matrimonial agent. Not a word passed. We were all failures in life, and could not trouble to dissemble it, in that heat. Moreover, we were used to each other, as types if not as persons, and had lost curiosity. So we sat listless, dispirited, drawing difficult breath and staring vacuously. The hope we shared in common—that nobody would claim the vacant seat—was too obvious to be discussed.

But at Charing Cross the twelfth passenger got in—a boy with a stick, and a bundle in a blue handkerchief. He was about thirteen; bound for the docks, we could tell at a glance, to sail on his first voyage; and, by the way he looked about, we could tell as easily that in stepping outside Charing Cross Station he had set foot on London stones for the first time. When we pulled up, he was standing on the opposite pavement with dazed eyes like a hare's, wondering at the new world—the hansoms, the yelling news-boys, the flower-women, the crowd pushing him this way and that, the ugly shopfronts, the hurry and stink and din of it all. Then, hailing our 'bus, he started to run across —faltered—almost dropped his bundle—was snatched by our conductor out of the path of a running hansom, and hauled on board. His eyelids were pink and swollen; but he was not crying, though he wanted to. Instead, he took a great gulp, as he pushed between our knees to his seat, and tried to look brave as a lion.

The passengers turned an incurious, half-resentful stare upon him, and then repented. 1

B 2

think that more than one of us wanted to speak,
but dared not.

It was not so much the little chap's look. But
to the knot of his sea-kit there was tied a bunch
of cottage-flowers—sweet williams, boy's love,
love-lies-bleeding, a few common striped carnations, and a rose or two—and the sight and
smell of them in that frowsy 'bus were like tears
on thirsty eyelids. We had ceased to pity what
we were, but the heart is far withered that
cannot pity what it has been; and it made us
shudder to look on the young face set towards
the road along which we had travelled so far.
Only the minor actress dropped a tear; but she
was used to expressing emotion, and half-way
down the Strand the 'bus stopped and she left
us.

The woman with an incurable complaint
touched me on the knee.

"Speak to him," she whispered.

But the whisper did not reach, for I was two
hundred miles away, and occupied in starting off
to school for the first time. I had two shillings
in my pocket; and at the first town where the

coach baited I was to exchange these for a coco-nut and a clasp-knife. Also, I was to break the knife in opening the nut, and the nut, when opened, would be sour. A sense of coming evil, therefore, possessed me.

"Why don't you speak to him?"

The boy glanced up, not catching her words, but suspicious: then frowned and looked defiant.

"Ah," she went on in the same whisper, "it's only the young that I pity. Sometimes, sir— for my illness keeps me much awake—I lie at night in my lodgings and listen, and the whole of London seems filled with the sound of children's feet running. Even by day I can hear them, at the back of the uproar——"

The matrimonial agent grunted and rose, as we halted at the top of Essex Street. I saw him slip a couple of half-crowns into the conductor's hand: and he whispered something, jerking his head back towards the interior of the 'bus. The boy was brushing his eyes, under pretence of putting his cap forward; and by the time he stole a look around to see if anyone had

observed, we had started again.   I pretended to
stare out of the window, but marked the wet
smear on his hand as he laid it on his lap.

In less than a minute it was my turn to
alight.   Unlike the matrimonial agent, I had
not two half-crowns to spare; but, catching the
sick woman's eye, forced up courage to nod and
say—

"Good luck, my boy."

"Good day, sir."

A moment after I was in the hot crowd,
whose roar rolled east and west for miles. And at
the back of it, as the woman had said, in street
and side-lane and blind-alley, I heard the foot-
fall of a multitude more terrible than an army
with banners, the ceaseless pelting feet of
children—of Whittingtons turning and turning
again.

FORTUNIO.

AT Tregarrick Fair they cook a goose in twenty-two different ways; and as no one who comes to the fair would dream of eating any other food, you may fancy what a reek of cooking fills the narrow grey street soon after mid-day.

As a boy, I was always given a holiday to go to the goose-fair; and it was on my way thither across the moors, that I first made Fortunio's acquaintance. I wore a new pair of corduroys, that smelt outrageously—and squeaked, too, as I trotted briskly along the bleak high road; for I had a bright shilling to spend, and it burnt a hole in my pocket. I was planning my purchases, when I noticed, on a windy eminence of the road ahead, a man's figure sharply defined against the sky.

He was driving a flock of geese, so slowly that I soon caught him up; and such a man or such geese I had never seen. To begin with, his rags were worse than a scarecrow's. In one hand he carried a long staff; the other held a small book close under his nose, and his lean shoulders bent over as he read in it. It was clear, from the man's undecided gait, that all his eyes were for this book. Only he would look up when one of his birds strayed too far on the turf that lined the highway, and would guide it back to the stones again with his staff. As for the geese, they were utterly draggle-tailed and stained with travel, and waddled, every one, with so woe-begone a limp that I had to laugh as I passed.

The man glanced up, set his forefinger between the pages of his book, and turned on me a long sallow face and a pair of the most beautiful brown eyes in the world.

" Little boy," he said, in a quick foreign way —"rosy little boy. You laugh at my geese, eh ? "

No doubt I stared at him like a ninny, for he went on—

" Little wide-mouthed Cupidon, how you gaze ! Also, by the way, how you smell ! "

" It's my corduroys," said I.

"Then I discommend your corduroys. But I approve your laugh. Laugh again—only at the right matter : laugh at this——"

And, opening his book again, he read a long passage as I walked beside him ; but I could make neither head nor tail of it.

"That is from the 'Sentimental Journey,' by Laurence Sterne, the most beautiful of your English wits. Ah, he is more than French ! Laugh at it."

It was rather hard to laugh thus to order ; but suddenly he set me the example, showing two rows of very white teeth, and fetching from his hollow chest a sound of mirth so incongruous with the whole aspect of the man, that I began to grin too.

"That's right ; but be louder. Make the sounds that you made just now——"

He broke off sharply, being seized with an ugly fit of coughing, that forced him to halt and lean on his staff for a while. When he recovered we walked on together after the geese, he talking all the way in high-flown sentences that were Greek to me, and I stealing a look every now and then at his olive face, and half inclined to take to my heels and run.

We came at length to the ridge where the road dives suddenly into Tregarrick. The town lies along a narrow vale, and looking down, we saw flags waving along the street and much smoke curling from the chimneys, and heard the church-bells, the big drum, and the confused mutterings and hubbub of the fair. The sun—for the morning was still fresh—did not yet pierce to the bottom of the valley, but fell on the hillside opposite, where cottage-gardens in parallel strips climbed up from the town to the moorland beyond.

"What is that?" asked the goose-driver, touching my arm and pointing to a dazzling spot on the slope opposite.

"That's the sun on the windows of Gardener Tonken's glass-house."

"Eh?—does he live there?"

"He's dead, and the garden's 'to let;' you can just see the board from here. But he didn't live there, of course. People don't live in glass-houses; only plants."

"That's a pity, little boy, for their souls' sakes. It reminds me of a story—by the way, do you know Latin? No? Well, listen to this:—if I can sell my geese to-day, perhaps I will hire that glass-house, and you shall come there on half holidays, and learn Latin. Now run ahead and spend your money."

I was glad to escape, and in the bustle of the fair quickly forgot my friend. But late in the afternoon, as I had my eyes glued to a peep-show, I heard a voice behind me cry "Little boy!" and turning, saw him again. He was without his geese.

"I have sold them," he said, "for £5; and I have taken the glass-house. The rent is only £3 a year, and I shan't live longer, so that leaves me money to buy books. I shall feed on the snails in the garden, making soup of them, for there is a beautiful stove in the glass-house. When is your next half-holiday?"

"On Saturday."

"Very well. I am going away to buy books; but I shall be back by Saturday, and then you are to come and learn Latin."

It may have been fear or curiosity, certainly it was no desire for learning, that took me to Gardener Tonken's glass-house next Saturday afternoon. The goose-driver was there to welcome me.

"Ah, wide-mouth," he cried; "I knew you would be here. Come and see my library."

He showed me a pile of dusty, tattered volumes, arranged on an old flower-stand.

"See," said he, "no sorrowful books, only Aristophanes and Lucian, Horace, Rabelais, Molière, Voltaire's novels, 'Gil Blas,' 'Don Quixote,' Fielding, a play or two of Shakespeare, a volume or so of Swift, Prior's Poems, and Sterne—that divine Sterne! And a Latin Grammar and Virgil for you, little boy. First. eat some snails."

But this I would not. So he pulled out two three-legged stools, and very soon I was trying to fix my wandering wits and decline *mensa.*

After this I came on every half-holiday for nearly a year. Of course the tenant of the glass-house was a nine days' wonder in the town.

A crowd of boys and even many grown men
and women would assemble and stare into the
glass-house while we worked; but Fortunio (he
gave no other name) seemed rather to like it
than not. Only when some wiseacres approached
my parents with hints that my studies with a
ragged man who lived on snails and garden-stuff
were uncommonly like traffic with the devil,
Fortunio, hearing the matter, walked over one
morning to our home and had an interview with
my mother. I don't know what was said; but I
know that afterwards no resistance was made to
my visits to the glass-house.

They came to an end in the saddest and
most natural way. One September afternoon I
sat construing to Fortunio out of the first book
of Virgil's "Æneid"—so far was I advanced;
and coming to the passage—

"Tum breviter Dido, vultum demissa, profatur" . . . . .
I had just rendered *vultum demissa* "with
downcast eyes," when the book was snatched
from me and hurled to the far end of the glass-
house. Looking up, I saw Fortunio in a trans-
port of passion.

"Fool—little fool! Will you be like all the commentators? Will you forget what Virgil has said and put your own nonsense into his golden mouth?"

He stepped across, picked up the book, found the passage, and then turning back a page or so, read out—

"Sæpta armis *solioque alte subnixa* resedit."

"*Alte! Alte!*" he screamed: "Dido sat on high: Æneas stood at the foot of her throne. Listen to this:—'Then Dido, bending down her gaze . . . '"

He went on translating. A rapture took him, and the sun beat in through the glass roof, and lit up his eyes. He was transfigured; his voice swelled and sank with passion, swelled again, and then, at the words—

"Quæ te tam læta tulerunt
Sæcula? Qui tanti talem genuere parentes?"

it broke, the Virgil dropped from his hand, and sinking down on his stool he broke into a wild fit of sobbing.

"Oh, why did I read it? Why did I read this sorrowful book?" And then checking his sobs, he put a handkerchief to his mouth, took it away, and looked up at me with dry eyes.

" Go away, little one, Don't come again : I am going to die very soon now."

I stole out, awed and silent, and went home. But the picture of him kept me awake that night, and early in the morning I dressed and ran off to the glass-house.

He was still sitting as I had left him.

" Why have you come ? " he asked, harshly. " I have been coughing. I am going to die."

" Then I'll fetch a doctor."

" No."

" A clergyman ? "

" No."

But I ran for the doctor.

Fortunio lived on for a week after this, and at length consented to see a clergyman. I brought the vicar, and was told to leave them alone together and come back in an hour's time.

When I returned, Fortunio was stretched quietly on the rough bed we had found for him. and the Vicar, who knelt beside it, was speaking softly in his ear.

As I entered on tiptoe, I heard—

" . . . in that kingdom shall be no weeping——"

"Oh, Parson," interrupted Fortunio, "that's bad. I'm so bored with laughing that the good God might surely allow a few tears."

The parish buried him, and his books went to pay for the funeral. But I kept the Virgil; and this, with the few memories that I impart to you, is all that remains to me of Fortunio.

THE OUTLANDISH LADIES.

A MILE beyond the fishing village, as you follow the road that climbs inland towards Tregarrick, the two tall hills to right and left of the coombe diverge to make room for a third, set like a wedge in the throat of the vale. Here the road branches into two, with a sign-post at the angle; and between the sign-post and the grey scarp of the hill there lies an acre of waste ground that the streams have turned into a marsh. This is Loose-heels. Long before I learnt the name's meaning, in the days when I trod the lower road with slate and satchel, this spot was a favourite of mine—but chiefly in July, when the monkey-flower was out, and the marsh aflame with it.

There was a spell in that yellow blossom with the wicked blood-red spots, that held me its mere slave. Also the finest grew in desperate places. So that, day after day, when July came round, my mother would cry shame on my small-clothes, and my father take exercise

C

upon them; and all the month I went tingling. They were pledged to "break me of it"; but they never did.   Now they are dead, and the flowers—the flowers last always, as Victor Hugo says.   When, after many years, I revisited the valley, the stream had carried the seeds half a mile below Loose-heels, and painted its banks with monkey-blossoms all the way.   But the finest, I was glad to see, still inhabited the marsh.

Now, it is rare to find this plant growing wild; for, in fact, it is a garden flower.   And its history here is connected with a bit of mud wall, ruined and covered with mosses and ragwort, that still pushed up from the swampy ground when I knew it, and had once been part of a cottage.   How a cottage came here, and how its inhabitants entered and went out, are questions past guessing; for the marsh hemmed it in on three sides, and the fourth is a slope of hill fit to break your neck.   But there was the wall, and here is the story.

One morning, near the close of the last

century, a small child came running down to
the village with news that the cottage, which
for ten years had stood empty, was let; there
was smoke coming out at the chimney, and an
outlandish lady walking in the garden. Being
catechised, he added that the lady wore bassomy
bows in her cap, and had accosted him in a
heathen tongue that caused him to flee, fearing
worse things. This being told, two women,
rulers of their homes, sent their husbands up
the valley to spy, who found the boy had spoken
truth.

Smoke was curling from the chimney, and
in the garden the lady was still moving about—
a small yellow creature, with a wrinkled but
pleasant face, white curls, and piercing black
eyes. She wore a black gown, cut low in the
neck, a white kerchief, and bassomy (or purplish)
bows in her cap as the child had stated. Just
at present she was busy with a spade, and
showed an ankle passing neat for her age, as
she turned up the neglected mould. When the
men plucked up gallantry enough to offer their
services, she smiled and thanked them in

c 2

broken English, but said that her small forces would serve.

So they went back to their wives; and their wives, recollecting that the cottage formed part of the glebe, went off to inquire of Parson Morth, "than whom," as the tablet to his memory relates, "none was better to castigate the manners of the age." He was a burly, hard-riding ruffian, and the tale of his great fight with Gipsy Ben in Launceston streets is yet told on the countryside.

Parson Morth wanted to know if he couldn't let his cottage to an invalid lady and her sister without consulting every wash-mouth in the parish.

"Aw, so there's two!" said one of them, nodding her head. "But tell us, Parson dear, ef 'tes fitty for two unmated women to come trapesing down in a po'shay at dead o' night, when all modest flesh be in their bed-gowns?"

Upon this the Parson's language became grossly indelicate, after the fashion of those days. He closed his peroration by slamming the front door on his visitors; and they went

down the hill "blushing" (as they said) "all over,
at his intimate words."

So nothing more was known of the strangers.
But it was noticed that Parson Morth, when he
passed the cottage on his way to meet or
market, would pull up his mare, and, if the outlandish lady were working in the garden, would
doff his hat respectfully.

"*Bon jour, Mamzelle Henriette*"—this was
all the French the Parson knew. And the lady
would smile back and answer in English.

"Good-morning, Parson Morth."

"And Mamzelle Lucille?"

"Ah, just the same, my God! All the day
stare—stare. If you had known her before!—
so be-eautiful, so gifted, *si bien élevée!* It is an
affliction: but I think she loves the flowers."

And the Parson rode on with a lump in his
throat.

So two years passed, during which Mademoiselle Henriette tilled her garden and turned
it into a paradise. There were white roses on
the south wall, and in the beds mignonette and

boy's-love, pansies, carnations, gillyflowers, sweet-
williams, and flaming great hollyhocks; above
all, the yellow monkey-blossoms that throve so
well in the marshy soil. And all that while no
one had caught so much as a glimpse of her
sister, Lucille. Also how they lived was a
marvel. The outlandish lady bought neither
fish, nor butcher's meat, nor bread. To be sure,
the Parson sent down a pint of milk every
morning from his dairy; the can was left at the
garden-gate and fetched at noon, when it was
always found neatly scrubbed, with the price of
the milk inside. Besides, there was a plenty of
vegetables in the garden.

But this was not enough to avert the whisper
of witchcraft. And one day, when Parson Morth
had ridden off to the wrestling matches at
Exeter, the blow fell.

Farmer Anthony of Carne — great-grand-
father of the present farmer—had been losing
sheep. Now, not a man in the neighbourhood would own to having stolen them; so
what so easy to suspect as witchcraft? Who
so fatally open to suspicion as the two out-

landish sisters? Men, wives, and children formed a procession.

The month was July; and Mademoiselle Henriette was out in the garden, a bunch of monkey-flowers in her hand, when they arrived. She turned all white, and began to tremble like a leaf. But when the spokesman stated the charge, there was another tale.

"It was an infamy. Steal! She would have them know that she and her sister were of good West Indian family—*très bien élevées.*" Then followed a torrent of epithets. They were *lâches* —*poltrons.* Why were they not fighting Bona- parte, instead of sending their wives up to the cliffs, dressed in red cloaks, to scare him away, while they bullied weak women?

They pushed past her. The cottage held two rooms on the ground floor. In the kitchen, which they searched first, they found only some garden-stuff and a few snails salted in a pan. There was a door leading to the inner room, and the foremost had his hand on it, when Made- moiselle Henriette rushed before him, and flung herself at his feet. The yellow monkey-blossoms were scattered and trampled on the floor.

"*Ah—non, non, messieurs! Je vous prie— Elle est si—si horrible!*"

They flung her down, and pushed on.

The invalid sister lay in an arm-chair with her back to the doorway, a bunch of monkey-flowers beside her. As they burst in, she started, laid both hands on the arms of her chair, and turned her face slowly upon them.

She was a leper!

They gave one look at that featureless face, with the white scales shining upon it, and ran back with their arms lifted before their eyes. One woman screamed. Then a dead stillness fell on the place, and the cottage was empty.

On the following Saturday Parson Morth walked down to the inn, just ten minutes after stalling his mare. He strode into the tap-room in his muddy boots, took two men by the neck, knocked their skulls together, and then demanded to hear the truth.

"Very well," he said, on hearing the tale;

" to-morrow I march every man Jack of you up to the valley, if it's by the scruff of your necks, and in the presence of both of those ladies—of *both*, mark you—you shall kneel down and ask them to come to church. I don't care if I empty the building. Your fathers (who were men, not curs) built the south transept for those same poor souls, and cut a slice in the chancel arch through which they might see the Host lifted. That's where *you* sit, Jim Trestrail, churchwarden; and by the Lord Harry, they shall have your pew."

He marched them up the very next morning. He knocked, but no one answered. After waiting a while, he put his shoulder against the door, and forced it in.

There was no one in the kitchen. In the inner room one sister sat in the arm-chair. It was Mademoiselle Henriette, cold and stiff. Her dead hands were stained with earth.

At the back of the cottage they came on a freshly-formed mound, and stuck on the top of it a piece of slate, such as children erect over a thrush's grave.

On it was scratched—

> *Ci-Gît*
> *LUCILLE,*
> *Jadis si Belle ;*
> *Dont dix-neuf Jeunes Hommes, Planteurs de*
> *SAINT DOMINGUE.*
> *ont demandé la Main.*
> *MAIS LA PETITE NE VOULAIT PAS.*
> *R. I. P.*

This is the story of Loose-heels, otherwise Lucille's.

STATEMENT OF GABRIEL FOOT, HIGHWAYMAN.

THE jury re-entered the court after half an hour's consultation.

It all comes back to me as vividly as though I stood in the dock at this very moment. The dense fog that hung over the well of the court; the barristers' wigs that bobbed up through it, and were drowned again in that seething cauldron; the rays of the guttering candles (for the murder-trial had lasted far into the evening) that loomed through it and wore a sickly halo; the red robes and red face of my lord judge opposite that stared through it and outshone the candles; the black crowd around, seen mistily; the voice of the usher calling "Silence!"; the shuffling of the jurymen's feet; the pallor on their faces as I leant forward and tried to read the verdict on them; the very smell of the place, compounded of fog, gaol-fever, the close air, and the dinners eaten earlier in the day by the crowd—all this strikes home upon me as sharply as it then did, after the numb apathy of waiting.

As the jury huddled into their places I stole a look at my counsel. He paused for a moment from his task of trimming a quill, shot a quick glance at the foreman's face, and then went on cutting as coolly as ever.

" Gentlemen of the jury "—it was the judge's voice—" are you agreed upon your verdict ? "

" We are."

" Do you find the prisoner guilty or not guilty ? "

" *Not guilty.*"

It must have been full a minute, as I leant back clutching the rail in front of me, before I saw anything but the bleared eyes of the candles, or heard anything but a hoarse murmur from the crowd. But as soon as the court ceased to heave, and I could stare about me, I looked towards my counsel again.

He was still shaping his pen. He made no motion to come forward and shake hands over my acquittal, for which he had worked un-

tiringly all day. He did not even offer to
speak. He just looked up, nodded carelessly,
and turned to his junior beside him; but in
that glance I had read something which turned
my heart cold, then sick, within me, and from
that moment my hatred of the man was as deep
as hell.

In the fog outside I got clear of the gaping
crowd, but the chill of the night after that
heated court pierced my very bones. I had
on the clothes I had been taken in. It was
June then, and now it was late in October. I
remember that on the day when they caught
me I wore my coat open for coolness. Four
months and a half had gone out of my life.
Well, I had money enough in my pocket to
get a greatcoat; but I must put something
warm inside me first, to get out the chill that
cursed lawyer had laid on my heart.

I had purposely chosen the by-lanes of the
town, but I remembered a certain tavern—the
"Lamb and Flag"—which lay down a side alley.
Presently the light from its windows struck

across the street, ahead. I pushed open the
door and entered.

The small bar was full of people newly come
from the court, and discussing the trial in all
its bearings. In the babel I heard a dozen
different opinions given in as many seconds.
and learnt enough, too, to make me content
with the jury I had had. But the warmth of
the place was pleasant, and I elbowed my way
forward to the counter.

There was a woman standing by the door as I
entered, who looked curiously at me for a moment,
then turned to nudge a man at her side, and
whisper. The whisper grew as I pressed forward, and before I could reach the counter a hand
was laid on my shoulder from behind. I turned.

" Well ? " said I.

It was a heavy-looking drover that had
touched me.

" Are you the chap that was tried to-day for
murder of Jeweller Todd ? " he asked

" Well ? " said I again, but I could see the
crowd falling back, as if I was a leper, at his
question.

"Well? 'T aint well then, as I reckon, to be making so free with respectable folk."

There was a murmur of assent from the mouths turned towards me. The landlord came forward from behind the bar.

"I was acquitted," I urged defiantly.

"Ac-quitted!" said he, with big scorn in the syllables. "Hear im now—'ac-quitted!' Landlord, is this a respectable house?"

The landlord gave his verdict.

"H'out yer goes, and damn yer impudence!"

I looked round, but their faces were all dead against me.

"H'out yer goes!" repeated the landlord. "And think yerself lucky it aint worse," added the drover.

With no further defence I slunk out into the night once more.

A small crowd of children (Heaven knows whence or how they gathered) followed me up the court and out into the street. Their numbers swelled as I went on, and some began to hoot and pelt me; but when I gained the top of the hill, and a lonelier district, I turned and struck among them with my stick. It did my heart good to hear their screams.

After that I was let alone, and tramped forward past the scattered houses, towards the open country and the moors. Up here there was scarcely any fog, but I could see it, by the rising moon, hanging like a shroud over the town below. The next town was near upon twelve miles off, but I do not remember that I thought of getting so far. I could not have thought at all, in fact, or I should hardly have taken the high-road upon which the jeweller had been stopped and murdered.

There was a shrewd wind blowing, and I shivered all over; but the cold at my heart was worse, and my hate of the man who had set it there grew with every step. I thought of the four months and more which parted the two lives of Gabriel Foot, and what I should make of the new one. I had my chance again— a chance gained for me beyond hope by that counsel but for whom I should be sleeping to-night in the condemned cell; a chance, and a good chance, but for that same cursed lawyer. Ugh! how cold it was, and how I hated *him* for it!

There was a little whitewashed cottage on the edge of the moorland just after the hedge-rows ceased—the last house before the barren heath began, standing a full three hundred yards from any other dwelling. Its front faced the road, and at the back an outhouse and a wretched garden jutted out on the waste land. There was a light in each of its windows to-night, and as I passed down the road I heard the dismal music of a flute.

Perhaps it was this that jogged my thoughts and woke them up to my present pass. At any rate, I had not gone more than twenty yards before I turned and made for the door. The people might give me a night's lodging in the outhouse; at any rate, they would not refuse a crust to stay the fast which I had not broken since the morning. I tapped gently with my knuckles on the door, and listened.

I waited five minutes, and no one answered. The flute still continued its melancholy tune; it was evidently in the hands of a learner, for

D

the air (a dispiriting one enough at the best)
kept breaking off suddenly and repeating itself.
But the performer had patience, and the sound
never ceased for more than two seconds at a
time.   Besides this, nothing could be heard.
The blinds were drawn in all the windows.
The glow of the candles through them was
cheerful enough, but nothing could be seen
of the house inside.   I knocked a second time,
and a third, with the same result.   Finally,
tired of this, I pushed open the low gate which
led into the garden behind, and stole round to
the back of the cottage.

Here, too, the window on the ground floor
was lit up behind its blinds, but that of the
room above was shuttered.   There was a hole
in the shutter, however, where a knot of the
wood had fallen out, and a thin shaft of light
stretched across the blackness and buried itself
in a ragged yew-tree at the end of the garden.
From the loudness of the sounds I judged this
to be the room where the flute-playing was
going on.   The crackling of my footsteps on
the thin soil did not disturb the performer, so

I gathered a handful of earth and pitched it up against the pane. The flute stopped for a minute or so, but just as I was expecting to see the shutter open, went on again : this time the air was " Pretty Polly Oliver."

I crept back again, and began to hammer more loudly at the door. " Come," said I, " whoever this may be inside, I'll see for myself at any rate," and with that I lifted the latch and gave the door a heavy kick. It flew open quite easily (it had not even been locked), and I found myself in a low kitchen. The room was empty, but the relics of supper lay on the deal table, and the remains of what must have been a noble fire were still smouldering on the hearthstone. A crazy, rusty blunderbuss hung over the fireplace. This, with a couple of rough chairs, a broken bacon-rack, and a small side-table, completed the furniture of the place. No; for as I sat down to make a meal off the remnants of supper, something lying on the lime-ash floor beneath this side-table caught my eye. I stepped forward and picked it up.

It was a barrister's wig.

D 2

"This is a queer business," thought I; and I laid it on the table opposite me as I went on with my supper. It was a "gossan" wig, as we call it in our parts; a wig grown yellow and rusty with age and wear. It looked so sly and wicked as it lay there, and brought back the events of the day so sharply that a queer dread took me of being discovered with it. I pulled out my pistol, loaded it (they had given me back both the powder and pistol found on me when I was taken), and laid it beside my plate. This done, I went on with my supper— it was an excellent cold capon—and all the time the flute up-stairs kept toot-tootling without stopping, except to change the tune. It gave me "Hearts of Oak," "Why, Soldiers, why?" "Like Hermit Poor," and "Come, Lasses and Lads," before I had fairly cleared the dish.

"And now," thought I, "I have had a good supper; but there are still three things to be done. In the first place I want drink, in the second I want a bed, and in the third I want to thank this kind person, whoever he is, for

his hospitality.   I'm not going to begin life
No. 2 with housebreaking."

I rose, slipped the pistol into my tail-pocket,
and followed the sound up the ramshackle stairs.
My footsteps made such a racket on their old
timbers as fairly to frighten me, but it never
disturbed the flute-player.   He had harked back
again to " Like Hermit Poor " by this time, and
the dolefulness of it was fit to make the dead
cry out, but he went whining on until I reached
the head of the stairs and struck a rousing
knock on the door.

The playing stopped.   " Come in," said a
cheery voice; but it gave me no cheerfulness.
Instead of that, it sent all the comfort of my
supper clean out of me, as I opened the door
and saw *him* sitting there.

There he was, the man who had saved my
neck that day, and whom most I hated in the
world, sitting before a snug fire, with his flute
on his knee, a glass of port wine at his elbow,
and looking so comfortable, with that knowing
light in his grey eyes, that I could have killed
him where he sat.

"Oh, it's you, is it?" he said, just the very least bit surprised and no more. "Come in."

I stood in the doorway hesitating.

"Don't stay letting in that monstrous draught, man; but sit down. You'll find the bottle on the table and a glass on the shelf."

I poured out a glassful and drank it off. The stuff was rare (I can remember its trick on the tongue to this day), but somehow it did not drive the cold out of my heart. I took another glass, and sat sipping it and staring from the fire to my companion.

He had taken up the flute again, and was blowing a few deep notes out of it, thoughtfully enough. He was a small, squarely-built man, with a sharp ruddy face like a frozen pippin, heavy grey eyebrows, and a mouth like a trap when it was not pursed up for that everlasting flute. As he sat there with his wig off, the crown of his bald head was fringed with an obstinate-looking patch of hair, the colour of a badger's. My amazement at finding him here at this hour, and alone, was lost in my hatred of the man as I saw the depths of complacent knowledge in his face. I felt that I must kill him sooner or later, and the sooner the better.

Presently he laid down his flute again and spoke :—

"I scarcely expected you."

I grunted something in answer.

"But I might have known something was up, if I'd only paid attention to my flute. It and I are not in harmony to-night. It doesn't like the secrets I've been blowing into it; it has heard a lot of queer things in its time, but it's an innocent-minded flute for all that, and I'm afraid that what I've told it to-night is a point beyond what it's prepared to go."

"I take it, it knows a damned deal too much," growled I.

He looked at me sharply for an instant, rose, whistled a bar or two of "Like Hermit Poor," reached down a couple of clay pipes from the shelf, filled one for himself, and gravely handed the other with the tobacco to me.

"Beyond what it is prepared to go," he echoed quietly, sinking back in his chair and puffing at the pipe. "It's a nice point that we have been discussing together, my flute and I, and I won't say but that I've got the worst of it. By the way, what do you mean to do now that you have a fresh start?"

Now I had not tasted tobacco for over four months, and its effect upon my wits was surprising. It seemed to oil my thoughts till they worked without a hitch, and I saw my plan of action marked out quite plainly before me.

"Do you want to know the first step of all?" I asked.

"To be sure; the first step at any rate determines the direction."

"Well then," said I, very steadily, and staring into his face, "the first step of all is that I am going to kill you."

"H'm," said he after a bit, and I declare that not so much as an eyelash of the man shook, "I thought as much. I guessed *that* when you came into the room. And what next?"

"Time enough then to think of 'what next,'" I answered; for though I was set upon blowing his brains out, I longed for him to blaze out into a passion and warm up my blood for the job.

"Pardon me," he said, as coolly as might be, "that would be the very worst time to think of it. For, just consider: in the first place you will already be committed to your way of life, and secondly, if I know anything about you, you would be far too much flurried for any thought worth the name."

There was a twinkle of frosty humour in his eye as he said this, and in the silence which followed I could hear him chuckling to himself, and tasting the words over again as though they were good wine. I sat fingering my pistol and waiting for him to speak again. When he did so, it was with another dry chuckle and a long puff of tobacco smoke.

"As you say, I know a deal too much. Shall I tell you how much?"

"Yes, you may if you'll be quick about it."

"Very well, then, I will. Do you mind passing the bottle? Thank you. I probably know not only too much, but a deal more than you guess. First let us take the case for the Crown.

The jeweller is travelling by coach at night over
the moors.   He has one postillion only, Roger
Tallis by name, and by character shady.   The
jeweller has money (he was a niggardly fool to
take only one postillion), and carries a diamond
of great, or rather of an enormous and notable
value (he was a bigger fool to take this).   In the
dark morning two horses come galloping back,
frightened and streaming with sweat.   A search
party goes out, finds the coach upset by the
Four Holed Cross, the jeweller lying beside it
with a couple of pistol bullets in him, and the
money, the diamond, and Roger Tallis—nowhere.   So much for the murdered man.   Two
or three days after, you, Gabriel Foot, by character also shady, and known to be a friend of
Roger Tallis, are whispered to have a suspicious
amount of money about you, also blood-stains
on your coat.   It further leaks out that you
were travelling on the moors afoot on the night
in question, and that your pistols are soiled with
powder.   Case for the Crown closes.   Have I
stated it correctly ? "

I nodded ; he took a sip or two at his wine,

laid down his pipe as if the tobacco spoiled
the taste of it, took another sip, and continued :—

"Case for the defence. That Roger Tallis
has decamped, that no diamond has been found
on you (or anywhere), and lastly that the
bullets in the jeweller's body do not fit your
pistols, but came from a larger pair. Not very
much of a case, perhaps, but this last is a strong
point."

"Well ? " I asked, as he paused.

"Now then for the facts of the case. Would
you oblige me by casting a look over there in
the corner ? "

"I see nothing but a pickaxe and shovel."

"Ha! very good; 'nothing but a pickaxe
and shovel.' Well, to resume: facts of the case
—Roger Tallis murders the jeweller, and you
murder Roger Tallis; after that, as you say,
'nothing but a pickaxe and shovel.'"

And with this, as I am a living sinner, the
rosy-faced old boy took up his flute and blew a
stave or two of "Come, Lasses and Lads."

"Did you dig him up?" I muttered hoarsely;

and although deathly cold I could feel a drop of sweat trickling down my forehead and into my eye.

" What, before the trial ?   My good sir, you have a fair, a very fair, aptitude for crime, but believe me, you have much to learn both of legal etiquette and of a lawyer's conscience." And for the first time since I came in I saw something like indignation on his ruddy face.

" Now," he continued, " I either know too much or not enough.   Obviously I know enough for you to wish, and perhaps wisely, to kill me. The question is, whether I know enough to make it worth your while to spare me.   I think I do; but that is for you to decide.   If I put you to-night, and in half an hour's time, in possession of property worth ten thousand pounds, will that content you ? "

" Come, come," I said, " you need not try to fool me, nor think I am going to let you out of my sight."

" You misunderstand. I desire neither; I only wish a bargain.   I am ready to pledge you my word to make no attempt to escape before you are in possession of that property, and to offer no resistance to your shooting me in case you fail to obtain it, provided on the other hand you pledge your word to spare my life should you succeed within half an hour. And, my dear sir, considering the relative value of your word and mine, I think it must be confessed you have the better of the bargain."

I thought for a moment. "Very well then," said I, " so be it; but if you fail——"

" I know what happens," replied he.

With that he blew a note or two on his flute, took it to pieces, and carefully bestowed it in the tails of his coat. I put away my pistol in mine.

"Do you mind shouldering that spade and pickaxe, and following me?" he asked. I took them up in silence. He drained his glass and put on his hat.

"Now I think we are ready. Stop a moment."

He reached across for the glass which I had emptied, took it up gingerly between thumb and forefinger, and tossed it with a crash on to the hearthstone. He then did the same to my pipe, after first snapping the stem into halves. This done, he blew out one candle, and with great gravity led the way down the staircase. I shouldered the tools and followed, while my heart hated him with a fiercer spite than ever.

We passed down the crazy stairs and through the kitchen. The candles were still burning there. As my companion glanced at the supper-table, " H'm," he said, "not a bad beginning of a new leaf. My friend, I will allow you exactly twelve months in which to get hanged."

I made no answer, and we stepped out into the night. The moon was now up, and the high-road stretched like a white ribbon into the gloom. The cold wind bore up a few heavy clouds from the north-west, but for the most part we could see easily enough. We trudged side by side along the road in silence, except that I could hear my companion every now and then whistling softly to himself.

As we drew near to the Four Holed Cross and the scene of the murder I confess to an uneasy feeling and a desire to get past the place

with all speed. But the lawyer stopped by the
very spot where the coach was overturned, and
held up a finger as if to call attention. It was a
favourite trick of his with the jury.

" This was where the jeweller lay. Some
fifteen yards off there was another pool of blood.
Now the jeweller must have dropped instantly
for he was shot through the heart. Yet no one
doubted but that the other pool of blood was
his. Fools ! "

With this he turned off the road at right
angles, and began to strike rapidly across the
moor. At first I thought he was trying to
escape me, but he allowed me to catch him up
readily enough, and then I knew the point for
which he was making. I followed doggedly.
Clouds began to gather over the moon's face,
and every now and then I stumbled heavily on
the uneven ground ; but he moved along nimbly
enough, and even cried " Shoo ! " in a sprightly
voice when a startled plover flew up before his
feet. Presently, after we had gone about five
hundred yards on the heath, the ground broke
away into a little hollow, where a rough track led

down to the Lime Kilns and the thinly wooded
stream that washed the valley below. We
followed this track for ten minutes or so, and
presently the masonry of the disused kilns
peered out, white in the moonlight, from
between the trees.

There were three of these kilns standing
close together beside the path; but my companion without hesitation pulled up almost
beneath the very arch of the first, peered about,
examined the ground narrowly, and then
motioned to me.

" Dig here."

" If we both know well enough what is
underneath, what is the use of digging ? "

" I very much doubt if we do," said he.
" You had better dig."

I can feel the chill creeping down my back
as I write of it; but at the time, though I well
knew the grisly sight which I was to discover, I
dug away steadily enough.   The man who had
surprised my secret set himself down on a dark
bank of ferns at about ten paces' distance, and

began to whistle softly, though I could see his fingers fumbling with his coat-tails as though they itched to be at the flute again.

The moon's rays shone fitfully upon the white face of the kiln, and lit up my work. The little stream rushed noisily below. And so, with this hateful man watching, I laid bare the lime-burnt remains of the comrade whom, almost five months before, I had murdered and buried there. How I had then cursed my luck because forced to hide his corpse away before I could return and search for the diamond I had failed to find upon his body! But as I tossed the earth and lime aside, and discovered my handiwork, the moon's rays were suddenly caught and reflected from within the pit, and I fell forward with a short gasp of delight.

For there, kindled into quick shafts and points of colour—violet, green, yellow, and fieriest red—lay the missing diamond among Roger's bones. As I clutched the gem a black shadow fell between the moon and me. I looked up. My companion was standing over

E

me, with the twinkle still in his eye and the flute in his hand.

"You were a fool not to guess that he had swallowed it. I hope you are satisfied with the bargain. As we are not, I trust, likely to meet again in this world, I will here bid you *Adieu*, though possibly that is scarcely the word to use. But there is one thing I wish to tell you. I owe you a debt to-night for having prevented me from committing a crime. You saw that I had the spade and pickaxe ready in the cottage. Well, I confess I lusted for that gem. I was arguing out the case with my flute when you came in."

"If," said I, "you wish a share——"

"Another word," he interrupted very gravely, "and I shall be forced to think that you insult me. As it is, I am grateful to you for supporting my flute's advice at an opportune moment. I will now leave you. Two hours ago I was in a fair way of becoming a criminal. I owe it to you, and to my flute, that I am still merely a lawyer. Farewell!"

With that he turned on his heel and was

gone with a swinging stride up the path and across the moor.   His figure stood out upon the sky-line for a moment, and then vanished.   But I could hear for some time the tootle-tootle of his flute in the distance, and it struck me that its note was unusually sprightly and clear.

THE RETURN OF JOANNA.

HIGH and low, rich and poor, in Troy Town there are seventy-three maiden ladies. Under this term, of course, I include only those who may reasonably be supposed to have forsworn matrimony. And of the seventy-three, the two Misses Lefanu stand first, as well from their age and extraction (their father was an Admiral of the Blue) as because of their house, which stands in Fore Street and is faced with polished Luxulyan granite—the same that was used for the famous Duke of Wellington's coffin in St. Paul's Cathedral.

Miss Susan Lefanu is eighty-five; Miss Charlotte has just passed seventy-six. They are extremely small, and Miss Bunce looks after them. That is to say, she dresses them of a morning, arranges their chestnut "fronts," sets their caps straight, and takes them down to breakfast. After dinner (which happens in the middle of the day) she dresses them again and

conducts them for a short walk along the Rope-
walk, which they call "the Esplanade." In the
evening she brings out the Bible and sets it the
right way up for Miss Susan, who begins to medi-
tate on her decease; then sits down to a game
of *écarté* with Miss Charlotte, who as yet has
not turned her thoughts upon mortality. At
ten she puts them to bed. Afterwards, "the
good Bunce"—who is fifty, looks like a grena-
dier, and wears a large mole on her chin—takes
up a French novel, fastened by a piece of
elastic between the covers of Baxter's "Saint's
Rest," and reads for an hour before retiring.
Her pay is fifty-two pounds a year, and her
attachment to the Misses Lefanu a matter of
inference rather than perception.

One morning in last May, at nine o'clock,
when Miss Bunce had just arranged the pair in
front of their breakfast-plates, and was sitting
down to pour out the tea, two singers came
down the street, and their voices—a man's and
a woman's—though not young, accorded very
prettily :—

" Citizens, toss your pens away !
For all the world is mad to-day—
         Cuckoo—cuckoo !
   The world is mad to-day."

"What unusual words for a pair of street
singers!" Miss Bunce murmured, setting down
the tea-pot. But as Miss Charlotte was busy
cracking an egg, and Miss Susan in a sort of
coma, dwelling perhaps on death and its terrors,
the remark went unheeded.

" Citizens, doff your coats of black,
  And dress to suit the almanack—
        Cuckoo—"

The voices broke off, and a rat-tat sounded
on the front door.

"Say that we never give to beggars, under
any circumstances," murmured Miss Susan,
waking out of her lethargy.

The servant entered with a scrap of crumpled
paper in her hand. "There was a woman at the
door who wished to see Miss Lefanu."

"Say that we never give——" Miss Susan
began again, fumbling with the note. "Bunce,

I have on my gold-rimmed spectacles, and cannot read with them, as you know. The black-rimmed pair must be up-stairs, on the——"

"How d'ye do, my dears?" interrupted a brisk voice. In the doorway stood a plump middle-aged woman, nodding her head rapidly. She wore a faded alpaca gown, patched here and there, a shawl of shepherd's plaid stained with the weather, and a nondescript bonnet. Her face was red and roughened, as if she lived much out of doors.

"How d'ye do?" she repeated "I'm Joanna."

Miss Bunce rose, and going discreetly to the window, pretended to gaze into the street. Joanna, as she knew, was the name of the old ladies' only step-sister, who had eloped from home twenty years before, and (it was whispered) had disgraced the family. As for the Misses Lefanu, being unused to rise without help, they spread out their hands as if stretching octaves on the edge of the table, and feebly stared.

"Joanna," began the elder, tremulously, "if you have come to ask charity——"

"Bless your heart, no! What put that into your head?" She advanced and took the chair which Miss Bunce had left, and resting her elbows on the table, regarded her sisters steadily. "What a preposterous age you both must be, to be sure! My husband's waiting for me outside."

"Your husband?" Miss Charlotte quavered.

"Why, of course. Did you suppose, because I ran away to act, that I wasn't an honest woman?" She stretched out her left hand; and there was a thin gold ring on her third finger. "He isn't much of an actor, poor dear. In fact, not to put too fine a point on it, he has been hissed off two-and-thirty stages in Great Britain alone. Indeed, he's the very worst actor I ever saw, although I don't tell him. But as a husband he's sublime."

"Are there——" Miss Charlotte began, and broke down. "Are there," she tried again, "are there—any—children?"

"Ah, my dear, if there were, I might be tempted to repent."

"Don't you?" jerked out Miss Bunce,

turning abruptly from the window. There was
a certain sharp emotion in the question, but her
face was in the shadow. Joanna regarded her
for a moment or two and broke into a laugh.

"My dears, I have been an actress and a
mother. I retain the pride of both,—though
my little one died at three months, and no
manager will engage me now, because I refuse
to act unless my husband has a part. Theoreti-
cally, he is the first of artists; in practice——
You were asking, however, if I repent. Well,
having touched the two chief prizes within a
woman's grasp, I hardly see how it is likely. I
perceive that the object of my visit has been
misinterpreted. To be frank, I came to gloat
over you."

"Your step-sisters are at least respectable,"
Miss Bunce answered.

"Let us grant that to be a merit," retorted
Joanna: "Do I understand you to claim the
credit of it?"

"They are very clean, though," she went on,
looking from one to the other, "and well pre-
served. Susan, I notice, shows signs of failing;

she has dropped her spectacles into the tea-
cup. But to what end, Miss——"

" Bunce."

" To what end, Miss Bunce, are you preserv-
ing them ? "

" Madam, when you entered the room I was
of your way of thinking. Book after book that
I read "—Miss Bunce blushed at this point—
" has displayed before me the delights of that
quick artistic life that you glory in following.
I have eaten out my heart in longing. But now
that I see how it coarsens a women—for it *is*
coarse to sneer at age, in spite of all you may
say about uselessness being no better for being
protracted over much time——"

" You are partly right," Joanna interrupted,
" although you mistake the accident for the
essence. I am only coarse when confronted by
respectability. Nevertheless, I am glad if I
reconcile you to your lot."

" But the point is," insisted Miss Bunce,
" that a lady *never* forgets herself."

" And you would argue that the being liable
to forget myself is only another development of

that very character by virtue of which I follow
Art. Ah, well "—she nodded towards her step-
sisters—" I ask you why they and I should be
daughters of one father ? "

She rose and stepped to the piano in the
corner. It was a tall Collard, shaped, above the
key-board, like a cupboard. After touching the
notes softly, to be sure they were in tune, she
drew over a chair, and fell to playing Schumann's
"*Warum?*" very tenderly. It was a tinkling
instrument, but perhaps her playing gained
pathos thereby, before such an audience. At
the end she turned round: there were tears in
her eyes.

"You used to play the 'Osborne Quadrilles'
very nicely," observed Miss Susan, suddenly.
"Your playing has become very—very——"

"Disreputable," suggested Joanna.

"Well, not exactly. I was going to say 'un-
intelligible.'"

"It's the same thing." She rose, kissed her
step-sisters, and walked out of the room without
a look at Miss Bunce.

"Poor Joanna!" observed Miss Susan, after

a minute's silence. "She has aged very much. I really must begin to think of my end."

Outside, in the street, Joanna's husband was waiting for her—a dark, ragged man, with a five-act expression of face.

"Don't talk to me for a while," she begged. "I have been among ghosts."

"Ghosts ?"

"They were much too dull to be real: and yet—— Oh, Jack, I feel glad for the first time that our child was taken! I might have left him there."

"What shall we sing ?" asked the man, turning his face away.

"Something pious," Joanna answered with an ugly little laugh, "since we want our dinner. The public has still enough honesty left to pity piety." She stepped out into the middle of the street, facing her sisters' windows, and began, the man's voice chiming in at the third bar—

"In the sweet by-and-bye
We shall meet on that be—yeautiful shore." . .

PSYCHE.

*"Among these million Suns how shall the
strayed Soul find her way back to earth?"*

THE man was an engine-driver, thick-set and
heavy, with a short beard grizzled at the edge,
and eyes perpetually screwed up, because his life
had run for the most part in the teeth of the
wind. The lashes, too, had been scorched off.
If you penetrated the mask of oil and coal-dust
that was part of his working suit, you found a
reddish-brown phlegmatic face, and guessed its
age at fifty. He brought the last down train
into Lewminster station every night at 9.45, took
her on five minutes later, and passed through
Lewminster again at noon, on his way back with
the Galloper, as the porters called it.

He had reached that point of skill at which
a man knows every pound of metal in a loco-
motive; seemed to feel just what was in his
engine the moment he took hold of the levers

and started up; and was expecting promotion.
While waiting for it, he hit on the idea of study-
ing a more delicate machine, and married a
wife. She was the daughter of a woman at
whose house he lodged, and her age was less
than half of his own. It is to be supposed he
loved her.

A year after their marriage she fell into low
health, and her husband took her off to Lewminster for fresher air. She was lodging alone
at Lewminster, and the man was passing Lewminster station on his engine, twice a day, at the
time when this tale begins.

People—especially those who live in the
West of England—remember the great fire at
the Lewminster Theatre; how, in the second
Act of the *Colleen Bawn*, a tongue of light shot
from the wings over the actors' heads; how, even
while the actors turned and ran, a sheet of fire
swept out on the auditorium with a roaring
wind, and the house was full of shrieks and
blind death; how men and women were turned
to a white ash as they rose from their seats, so

fiercely the flames outstripped the smoke. These things were reported in the papers, with narratives and ghastly details, and for a week all England talked of Lewminster.

This engine-driver, as the 9.45 train neared Lewminster, saw the red in the sky. And when he rushed into the station and drew up, he saw that the country porters who stood about were white as corpses.

" What fire is that ? " he asked one.

" 'Tis the theayter ! There's a hundred burnt a'ready, and the rest treadin' each other's lives out while we stand talkin', to get 'pon the roof and pitch theirselves over ! "

Now the engine-driver's wife was going to the play that night, and he knew it. She had met him at the station, and told him so, at midday.

But there was nobody to take the train on, if he stepped off the engine; for his fireman was a young hand, and had been learning his trade for less than three weeks.

So when the five minutes were up---or

F

rather, ten, for the porters were bewildered that night—this man went on out of the station into the night. Just beyond the station the theatre was plain to see, above the hill on his left, and the flames were leaping from the roof; and he knew that his wife was there. But the train was never taken down more steadily, nor did a single passenger guess what manner of man was driving it.

At Drakeport, where his run ended, he stepped off the engine, walked from the railway-sheds to his mother-in-law's, where he still lodged, and went up-stairs to his bed without alarming a soul.

In the morning, at the usual hour, he was down at the station again, washed and cleanly dressed. His fireman had the Galloper's engine polished, fired up, and ready to start.

"Mornin'," he nodded, and looking into his driver's eyes, dropped the handful of dirty lint with which he had been polishing. After shuffling from foot to foot for a minute, he ended by climbing down on the far side of the engine.

"Oldster," he said, "'tis mutiny p'raps; but

s'help me, if I ride a mile 'longside that new
face o' your'n ! "

" Maybe you're right," his superior answered
wearily. " You'd best go up to the office, and
get somebody sent down i' my place. And
while you're there, you might get me a third-
class for Lewminster."

So this man travelled up to Lewminster as
passenger, and found his young wife's body
among the two score stretched in a stable-yard
behind the smoking theatre, waiting to be
claimed. And the day after the funeral he left
the railway company's service. He had saved
a bit, enough to rent a small cottage two miles
from the cemetery where his wife lay. Here he
settled and tilled a small garden beside the high-
road.

Nothing seemed to be wrong with the man
until the late summer, when he stood before the
Lewminster magistrates charged with a violent
and curiously wanton assault.

It appeared that one dim evening, late in
August, a mild gentleman, with Leghorn hat,

F 2

spectacles, and a green gauze net, came saunter-
ing by the garden where the ex-engine-driver
was pulling a basketful of scarlet runners: that
the prisoner had suddenly dropped his beans,
dashed out into the road, and catching the mild
gentleman by the throat had wrenched the
butterfly net from his hand and belaboured him
with the handle till it broke.

There was no defence, nor any attempt at
explanation. The mild gentleman was a stranger
to the neighbourhood. The magistrates mar-
velled, and gave his assailant two months.

At the end of that time the man came out of
gaol and went quietly back to his cottage.

Early in the following April he conceived a
wish to build a small greenhouse at the foot of
his garden, by the road, and spoke to the local
mason about it. One Saturday afternoon the
mason came over to look at the ground and dis-
cuss plans. It was bright weather, and while
the two men talked a white butterfly floated past
them—the first of the year.

Immediately the mason broke off his sentence and began to chase the butterfly round the garden: for in the West country there is a superstition that if a body neglect to kill the first butterfly he may see for the season, he will have ill luck throughout the year. So he dashed across the beds, hat in hand.

"I'll hat 'en—I'll hat 'en! No, fay! I'll miss 'en, I b'lieve. Shan't be able to kill 'n if her's wunce beyond th' gaate—stiddy, my son! Wo-op!"

Thus he yelled, waving his soft hat: and the next minute was lying stunned across a carrot-bed, with eight fingers gripping the back of his neck and two thumbs squeezing on his wind-pipe.

There was another assault case heard by the Lewminster bench; and this time the ex-engine-driver received four months. As before, he offered no defence: and again the magistrates were possessed with wonder.

Now the explanation is quite simple. This man's wits were sound, save on one point. He believed—why, God alone knows, who enabled him to drive that horrible journey without a tremor of the hand—that his wife's soul haunted him in the form of a white butterfly or moth. The superstition that spirits take this shape is not unknown in the West; and I suppose that as he steered his train out of the station, this fancy, by some odd freak of memory, leaped into his brain, and held it, hour after hour, while he and his engine flew forward and the burning theatre fell further and further behind. The truth was known a fortnight after his return from prison, which happened about the time of barley harvest.

A harvest-thanksgiving was held in the parish where he lived; and he went to it, being always a religious man. There were sheaves and baskets of vegetables in the chancel; fruit and flowers on the communion-table, with twenty-one tall candles burning above them; a processional hymn; and a long sermon. During the sermon, as the weather was hot and close, someone opened the door at the west end.

And when the preacher was just making up

his mind to close the discourse, a large white moth fluttered in at the west door.

There was much light throughout the church; but the great blaze came, of course, from the twenty-one candles upon the altar. And towards this the moth slowly drifted, as if the candles sucked her nearer and nearer, up between the pillars of the nave, on a level with their capitals. Few of the congregation noticed her, for the sermon was a stirring one; only one or two children, perhaps, were interested— and the man I write of. He saw her pass over his head and float up into the chancel. He half-rose from his chair.

" My brothers," said the preacher, " if two sparrows, that are sold for a farthing, are not too little for the care of this infinite Providence——"

A scream rang out and drowned the sentence. It was followed by a torrent of vile words, shouted by a man who had seen, now for the second time, the form that clothed his wife's soul shrivelled in unthinking flames. All that was left of the white moth lay on the altar-cloth, among the fruit at the base of the tallest candle-stick.

And because the man saw nothing but cruelty in the Providence of which the preacher spoke, he screamed and cursed, till they over-powered him and took him forth by the door, He was wholly mad from that hour.

THE COUNTESS OF BELLARMINE.

FEW rivers in England are without their "Lovers' Leap"; but the tradition of this one is singular, I believe. It overhangs a dark pool, midway down a west country valley—a sheer escarpment of granite, its lip lying but a stone's throw from the high-road, that here finds its descent broken by a stiff knoll, over which it rises and topples again like a wave.

I had drawn two shining peel out of the pool, and sat eating my lunch on the edge of the Leap, with my back to the road. Forty feet beneath me the water lay black and glossy, behind the dotted foliage of a birch-tree. My rod stuck upright from the turf at my elbow, and, whenever I turned my head, neatly bisected the countenance and upper half of Seth Truscott, an indigenous gentleman of miscellaneous habits and a predatory past, who had followed me that morning to carry the landing-net.

It was he who, after lunch, imparted the
story of the rock on which we sat; and as it
seemed at the time to gain somewhat by the
telling, I will not risk defacing it by meddling
with his dialect.

"I reckon, sir," he began, with an upward
nod at a belt of larches, the fringe of a great
estate, that closed the view at the head of the
vale, "you'm too young to mind th' ould Earl
o' Bellarmine, that owned Castle Cannick, up
yonder, in my growin' days. 'Ould Wounds'
he was nick-named—a cribbage-faced, what-the-
blazes kind o' varmint, wi' a gossan wig an' a
tongue like oil o' vitriol. He'd a-led the fore-
half o' his life, I b'lieve, in London church-town,
by reason that he an' his father couldn' be left
in a room together wi'out comin' to fisticuffs:
an' by all accounts was fashion's favourite in the
naughty city, doin' his duty in that state o' life
an' playing Hamlet's ghost among the Ten
Commandments.

"The upshot was that he killed a young
gentleman over a game o' whist, an' that was

too much even for the Londoners. So he packed
up and sailed for furrin' parts, an' didn' show his
face in England till th' ould man, his father, was
took wi' a seizure an' went dead, bein' palsied
down half his face, but workin' away to the end
at the most lift-your-hair wickedness wi' the
sound side of his mouth.

"Then the new Earl turned up an' settled at
Castle Cannick. He was a wifeless man, an', by
the look o't, had given up all wish to coax the
female eye: for he dressed no better 'n a jockey,
an' all his diversion was to ride in to Tregarrick
Market o' Saturdays, an' hang round the doorway o' the Pack-Horse Inn, by A. Walters, and
glower at the men an' women passin' up and
down the Fore Street, an' stand drinkin' brandy
an' water while the horse-jockeys there my-
lord'ed 'en. Two an' twenty glasses, they say,
was his quantum between noon an' nine o'clock;
an' then he'd climb into saddle an' ride home
to his jewelled four-poster, cursin' an' mutterin',
but sittin' his mare like a man of iron.

"But one o' these fine market-days he did a
thing that filled the mouths o' the country-side.

" He was loafin' by the Pack-Horse door, just as usual, at two o'clock, rappin' the head o' his crop on the side o' his ridin' boots, drawin' his brows down an' lookin' out curses from under 'em across the street to the saddler's opposite, when two drover-chaps came up the pavement wi' a woman atween 'em.

" The woman—or maid, to call her by her proper title—was a dark-browed slut, wi' eyes like sloes, an' hair dragged over her face till she looked like an owl in an ivy-bush. As for the gown o' her, 'twas no better 'n a sack tied round the middle, wi' a brave piece torn away by the shoulder, where one o' the men had clawed her.

" There was a pretty dido goin' on atween the dree, an' all talkin' together—the two men mobbin' each other, an' the girl i' the middle callin' em every name but what they was chris'ened, wi'out distinction o' persons, as the word goes.

" ' What's the uproar ? ' asks Ould Wounds, stoppin' the tap-tap o' his crop, as they comes up.

" ' The woman b'longs to me,' says the first. ' I've engaged to make her my lawful wife ; an'

I won't go from my word under two gallon o'
fourpenny.'

" ' You agreed to hand her over for one
gallon, first along,' says t'other, ' an' a bargain's
a bargain.'

" Says the woman, ' You're a pair o' hair-
splitting shammicks, the pair of 'ee. An' how
much beer be I to have for my weddin'
portion ? ' (says she)—'for that's all *I* care
about, one way or t'other.'

" Now Ould Wounds looked at the woman ;
an' 'tis to be thought he found her eyeable, for
he axed up sharp—

" ' Would 'ee kick over these two, an' marry
me, for a bottle o' gin ? '

" ' That would I.'

" ' An' to be called My Lady—Countess o'
Bellarmine ? '

" ' Better an' better.'

" ' I shall whack 'ee.'

" ' I don't care.'

" ' I shall kick an' cuff an' flog 'ee like a
span'el dog,' says he : ' by my body ! I shall make
'ee repent.'

" ' Give 'ee leave to try,' says she.

" An' that's how th' Earl o' Bellarmine courted his wife. He took her into the bar an' treated her to a bottle o' gin on the spot. At nine o'clock that evenin' she tuk hold of his stirrup-leather an' walked beside 'en, afoot, up to Castle Cannick. Next day, their banns were axed in church, an' in dree weeks she was My Ladyship.

" 'Twas a battle-royal that began then. Ould Wounds dressed the woman up to the nines, an' forced all the bettermost folk i' the county to pay their calls an' treat her like one o' the blood ; and then, when the proud guests stepped into their chariots an' druv away, he'd fall to, an' lick her across the shoulders wi' his ridin'-whip, to break her sperrit. 'Twas the happiest while o' th' ould curmudgeon's life, I do b'lieve ; for he'd found summat he cudn' tame in a hurry. There was a noble pond afore the house, i' those days, wi' urns an' heathen gods around the brim, an' twice he dragged her through it in her night-gown, I've heerd, an' always dined wi' a pistol laid by his plate, alongside the knives an' prongs, to scare her. But not she!

"An' next he tried to burn her in her bed: an' that wasn' no good.

"An' last of all he fell i' love wi' her: an' that broke her.

"One day—the tale goes—she made up her mind an' ordered a shay an' pair from the Pack-Horse. The postillion was to be waitin' by the gate o' the deer-park—the only gate that hadn't a lodge to it—at ten o'clock that night. 'Twas past nine afore dinner was done, an' she got up from her end o' the table an' walked across to kiss th' ould fellow. He, 'pon his side, smiled on her, pleased as Punch; for 'twas little more'n a fortni't since he'd discovered she was the yapple of his eye. She said 'Good night' an' went up-stairs to pack a few things in a bag, he openin' the door and shuttin' it upon her. Then he outs wi' his watch, waits a couple o' minutes, an' slips out o' the house.

"At five minutes to ten comes my ladyship,

glidin' over the short turf o' the deer-park, an'
glancin' over her shoulder at the light in his
lordship's libery window. 'Twas burnin' in true
watch-an'-fear-nothin' style, an' there, by the
gate, was the shay and horses, and postillion,
wrapped up and flapping his arms for warmth,
who touched his cap and put down the steps
for her.

"'Drive through Tregarrick,' says she, 'an'
don't spare whip-cord.'

"Slam went the door, up climbed the postillion, an' away they went like a house afire.
There was half-a-moon up an' a hoar frost
gatherin', an' my lady, leanin' back on the
cushions, could see the head and shoulders of
the postillion bob-bobbing, till it seemed his
head must work loose and tumble out of his
collar.

"The road they took, sir, is the same that
runs down the valley afore our very eyes. An'
'pon the brow o't, just when it comes in sight,
the off horse turned restive. In a minute 'twas
as much as the post-boy could ha' done to hold
'en. *But he didn' try.* Instead, he fell to

floggin' harder, workin' his arm up an' down like a steam-engin'.

" ' What the jiminy are 'ee doin ? ' calls out her ladyship—or words to that effec'—clutchin' at the side o' the shay, an' tryin' to stiddy hersel'.

" ' I thought I wasn' to spare whip-cord,' calls back the post-boy.

" An' with that he turned i' the saddle; an' 'twas the face o' her own wedded husband, as ghastly white as if 't burned a'ready i' the underground fires.

" Seein' it, her joints were loosed, an' she sat back white as he; an' down over the hill they swung at a breakneck gallop, shay lurchin' and stones flyin'.

" About thirty yards from where we'm sittin', sir, Ould Wounds caught the near rein twice round his wrist an lean't back, slowly pullin' it, till his face was slewed round over his left shoulder an' grinnin' in my lady's face.

" An' that was the last look that passed atween 'em. For now feeling the wheels on grass and the end near, he loosed the rein and fetched the horse he rode a cut atween the

G

ears—an' that's how 'twas," concluded Seth,
lamely.

Like most inferior narrators, he shied at the
big fence, flinched before the climax.   But as he
ended, I flung a short glance downward at the
birches and black water, and took up my rod
again with a shiver.

FROM

A COTTAGE IN TROY.

I.—A HAPPY VOYAGE.

THE cottage that I have inhabited these six years looks down on the one quiet creek in a harbour full of business. The vessels that enter beneath Battery Point move up past the grey walls and green quay-doors of the port to the jetties where their cargoes lie. All day long I can see them faring up and down past the mouth of my creek; and all the year round I listen to the sounds of them—the dropping or lifting of anchors, the *wh-h-ing!* of a siren-whistle cutting the air like a twanged bow, the concertina that plays at night, the rush of the clay cargo shot from the jetty into the lading ship. But all this is too far remote to vex me. Only one vessel lies beneath my terrace; and she has lain there for a dozen years. After many voyages she was purchased by the Board of Guardians in our district, dismasted, and anchored up here to serve as a hospital-ship in case the cholera visited us. She has never had a sick man on board from that day to the present. But once upon a time three people spent a very happy night on her deck, as you shall hear. She is called *The Gleaner*.

I think I was never so much annoyed in my life as on the day when Annie, my only servant, gave me a month's "warning." That was four years ago; and she gave up cooking for me to marry a young watchmaker down at the town— a youth of no mark save for a curious distortion of the left eyebrow (due to much gazing through a circular glass into the bowels of watches), a frantic assortment of religious convictions, a habit of playing the fiddle in hours of ease, and an absurd name—Tubal Cain Bonaday. I noticed that Annie softened it to " Tubey."

Of course I tried to dissuade her, but my arguments were those of a wifeless man, and very weak. She listened to them with much patience, and went off to buy her wedding-frock. She was a plain girl, without a scintilla of humour; and had just that sense of an omelet that is vouchsafed to one woman in a generation.

So she and Tubal Cain were married at the end of the month, and disappeared on their honeymoon, no one quite knew whither. They went on the last day of April.

At half-past eight in the evening of May 6th I had just finished my seventh miserable dinner. My windows were open to the evening, and the scent of the gorse-bushes below the terrace hung heavily underneath the verandah and stole into the room where I sat before the white cloth, in the lamp-light. I had taken a cigarette and was reaching for the match-box when I chanced to look up, and paused to marvel at a singular beauty in the atmosphere outside.

It seemed a final atonement of sky and earth in one sheet of vivid blue. Of form I could see nothing; the heavens, the waters of the creek below, the woods on the opposite shore were simply indistinguishable—blotted out in this one colour. If you can recall certain advertisements of Mr. Reckitt, and can imagine one of these transparent, with a soft light glowing behind it, you will be as near as I can help you to guessing the exact colour. And, but for a solitary star and the red lamp of a steamer lying off the creek's mouth, this blue covered the whole firmament and face of the earth.

I lit my cigarette and stepped out upon the verandah. In a minute or so a sound made me return, fetch a cap from the hall, and descend the terrace softly.

My feet trod on bluebells and red-robins, and now and then crushed the fragrance out of a low-lying spike of gorse. I knew the flowers were there, though in this curious light I could only see them by peering closely. At the foot of the terrace I pulled up and leant over the oak fence that guarded the abrupt drop into the creek.

There was a light just underneath. It came from the deck of the hospital ship, and showed me two figures standing there—a woman leaning against the bulwarks, and a man beside her. The man had a fiddle under his chin, and was playing " Annie Laurie," rather slowly and with a deal of sweetness.

When the melody ceased, I craned still further over the oak fence and called down,

"Tubal Cain!"

The pair gave a start, and there was some whispering before the answer came up to me.

"Is that you, sir?"

"To be sure," said I. "What are you two about on board *The Gleaner?*"

Some more whispering followed, and then Tubal Cain spoke again—

"It doesn't matter now, sir. We've lived aboard here for a week, and to-night's the end of our honeymooning. If 'tis no liberty sir, Annie's wishful that you should join us."

Somehow, the invitation, coming through this mysterious atmosphere, seemed at once natural and happy. The fiddle began again as I stepped away from the fence and went down to get my boat out. In three minutes I was afloat, and a stroke or two brought me to the ship's ladder. Annie and Tubal Cain stood at the top to welcome me.

But if I had felt no incongruity in paying

this respectful visit to my ex-cook and
her lover, I own that her appearance made
me stare. For, if you please, she was
dressed out like a lady, in a gown of pale blue
satin trimmed with swansdown—a low-necked
gown, too, though she had flung a white shawl
over her shoulders. Imagine this and the flood
of blue light around us, and you will hardly
wonder that, half-way up the ladder, I paused to
take breath. Tubal Cain was dressed as usual,
and tucking his fiddle under his arm, led me up
to shake hands with his bride as if she were a
queen. I cannot say if she blushed. Certainly
she received me with dignity : and then, invert-
ing a bucket that lay on the deck, seated
herself; while Tubal Cain and I sat down on the
deck facing her, with our backs against the
bulwarks.

"It's just this, sir," explained the bridegroom,
laying his fiddle across his lap, and speaking as
if in answer to a question : " it's just this :—by
trade you know me for a watchmaker, and for a
Plymouth Brother by conviction. All the week
I'm bending over a counter, and every Sabbath-

day I speak in prayer-meeting what I hold, that
life's a dull pilgrimage to a better world. If you
ask me, sir, to-night, I ought to say the same.
But a man may break out for once; and when
so well as on his honeymoon? For a week I've
been a free heathen: for a week I've been hiding
here, living with the woman I love in the open
air; and night after night for a week Annie here
has clothed herself like a woman of fashion. Oh,
my God! it has been a beautiful time—a happy
beautiful time that ends to-night!"

He set down the fiddle, crooked up a knee
and clasped his hands round it, looking at Annie.

"Annie, girl, what is it that we believe till
to-morrow morning? You believe—eh?—that
'tis a rare world, full of delights, and with no
ugliness in it?"

Annie nodded.

"And you love every soul—the painted
woman in the streets no less than your own
mother?"

Annie nodded again. "I'd nurse 'em both
if they were sick," she said.

"One like the other?"

"No difference."

"And there's nothing shames you?" Here he rose and took her hand. "You wouldn't blush to kiss me before master here?"

"Why should I?" She gave him a sober kiss, and let her hand rest in his.

I looked at her. She was just as quiet as in the old days when she used to lay my table. It was like gazing at a play.

I should be ashamed to repeat the nonsense that Tubal Cain thereupon began to talk; for it was mere midsummer madness. But I smoked four pipes contentedly while the sound of his voice continued, and am convinced that he never performed so well at prayer-meeting. Down at the town I heard the church-clock striking midnight, and then one o'clock; and was only aroused when the youth started up and grasped his fiddle.

"And now, sir, if you would consent to one thing, 'twould make us very happy. You can't play the violin, worse luck; but you might take a step or two round the deck with Annie, if I strike up a waltz-tune for you to move to."

It was ridiculous, but as he began to play I moved up to Annie, put my arm around her, and we began to glide round and round on the deck. Her face was turned away from mine, and looked over my shoulder; if our eyes had met, I am convinced I must have laughed or wept. It was half farce, half deadly earnest, and for me as near to hysterics as a sane man can go. Tubal Cain, that inspired young Plymouth Brother, was solemn as a judge. As for Annie, I would give a considerable amount, at this moment, to know what she thought of it. But she stepped very lightly and easily, and I am not sure I ever enjoyed a waltz so much. The blue light—that bewitching, intoxicating blue light—paled on us as we danced. The grey conquered it, and I felt that when we looked at each other the whole absurdity would strike us, and I should never be able to face these lovers again without a furious blush. As the day crept on, I stole a glance at Tubal Cain. He was scraping away desperately—*with his eyes shut.* For us the dance had become weariness, but we went on and on. We were afraid to halt.

Suddenly a string of the violin snapped. We stopped, and I saw Tubal Cain's hand pointing eastward. A golden ripple came dancing down the creek, and, at the head of the combe beyond, the sun's edge was mounting.

"Morning!" said the bridegroom.

"It's all done," said Annie, holding out a hand to me, without looking up. "And thank you, sir."

"We danced through the grey," I answered; and that was all I could find to say, as I stepped towards the ladder.

Half an hour later as I looked out of window before getting into bed I saw in the sunlight a boat moving down the creek towards the town Tubal Cain was rowing, and Annie sat in the stern. She had changed her gown.

They have been just an ordinary couple ever since, and attend their chapel regularly. Sometimes Annie comes over to make me an omelet; and, as a matter of fact, she is now in the kitchen. But not a word has ever been spoken between us about her honeymoon.

II.—THESE-AN'-THAT'S WIFE.

In the matter of These-an'-That himself, public opinion in Troy is divided. To the great majority he appears scandalously careless of his honour; while there are just six or seven who fight with a suspicion that there dwells something divine in the man.

To reach the town from my cottage I have to cross the Passage Ferry, either in the smaller boat which Eli pulls single-handed, or (if a market-cart or donkey, or drove of cattle be waiting on the slip) I must hang about till Eli summons his boy to help him with the horse-boat. Then the gangway is lowered, the beasts are driven on board, the passengers follow at a convenient distance, and the long sweeps take us slowly across the tide. It was on such a voyage, a few weeks after I settled in the neighbourhood, that I first met These-an'-That.

I was leaning back against the chain, with my cap tilted forward to keep off the dazzle of the June sunshine on the water, and lazily watching Eli as he pushed his sweep. Suddenly I grew aware that by frequent winks and jerks of the head he wished to direct my attention to a passenger on my right—a short, round man in black, with a basket of eggs on his arm.

There was quite a remarkable dearth of feature on this passenger's face, which was large, soft, and unhealthy in colour : but what surprised me was to see, as he blinked in the sunlight, a couple of big tears trickle down his cheeks and splash among the eggs in his basket.

"There's trouble agen, up at Kit's," remarked Eli, finishing his stroke with a jerk, and speaking for the general benefit, though the words were particularly addressed to a drover opposite.

"Ho ? " said the drover: " that woman agen ? "

The passengers, one and all, bent their eyes on the man in black, who smeared his face with his cuff, and began weeping afresh, silently.

"Beat en blue las' night, an' turned en to doors—the dirty trollop."

"Eli, don't 'ee——" put in the poor man, in a low, deprecating voice.

"Iss, an' no need to tell what for," exclaimed a red-faced woman who stood by the drover, with two baskets of poultry at her feet. "She's a low lot; a low trapesin' baggage. If These-an'-That, there, wasn' but a poor, ha'f-baked shammick, he'd ha' killed that wife o' his afore this."

"Naybours, I'd as lief you didn't mention it," appealed These-an'-That, huskily.

"I'm afeard you'm o' no account, These-an'-That: but sam-sodden, if I may say so," the drover observed.

"Put in wi' the bread, an' took out wi' the cakes," suggested Eli.

"Wife!—a pretty loitch, she an' the whole kit, up there!" went on the market-woman. "If you durstn't lay finger 'pon your wedded wife, These-an'-That, but let her an' that long-legged gamekeeper turn'ee to doors, you must be no better 'n a worm,—that's all I say."

H

I saw the man's face twitch as she spoke of the gamekeeper. But he only answered in the same dull way.

" I'd as lief you didn' mention it, friends,— if 'tis all the same."

His real name was Tom Warne, as I learnt from Eli afterwards; and he lived at St. Kit's, a small fruit-growing hamlet two miles up the river, where his misery was the scandal of the place. The very children knew it, and would follow him in a crowd sometimes, pelting him with horrible taunts as he slouched along the road to the kitchen garden out of which he made his living. He never struck one; never even answered; but avoided the school-house as he would a plague; and if he saw the Parson coming would turn a mile out of his road.

The Parson had called at the cottage a score of times at least: for the business was quite intolerable. Two evenings out of the six, the long-legged gamekeeper, who was just a big, drunken bully, would swagger easily into These-an'-That's kitchen and sit himself down without

so much as " by your leave." " Good evenin',
gamekeeper," the husband would say in his dull,
nerveless voice. Mostly he only got a jeer in
reply. The fellow would sit drinking These-
an'-That's cider and laughing with These-an'-
That's wife, until the pair, very likely, took too
much, and the woman without any cause broke
into a passion, flew at the little man, and drove
him out of doors, with broomstick or talons,
while the gamekeeper hammered on the table
and roared at the sport. His employer was an
absentee who hated the Parson, so the Parson
groaned in vain over the scandal.

Well, one Fair-day I crossed in Eli's boat
with the pair. The woman—a dark gipsy
creature—was tricked out in violet and yellow,
with a sham gold watch-chain and great alu-
minium earrings : and the gamekeeper had
driven her down in his spring-cart. As Eli
pushed off, I saw a small boat coming down
the river across our course. It was These-an'-
That, pulling down with vegetables for the fair.
I cannot say if the two saw him : but he glanced

H 2

up for a moment at the sound of their laughter,
then bent his head and rowed past us a trifle
more quickly. The distance was too great to
let me see his face.

I was the last to step ashore. As I waited
for Eli to change my sixpence, he nodded after
the couple, who by this time had reached the
top of the landing-stage, arm in arm.

" A bad day's work for *her*, I reckon."

It struck me at the moment as a moral
reflection of Eli's, and no more. Late in the
afternoon, however, I was enlightened.

In the midst of the Fair, about four o'clock,
a din of horns, beaten kettles, and hideous yelling, broke out in Troy. I met the crowd in
the main street, and for a moment felt afraid
of it. They had seized the woman in the tap-
room of the " Man-o'-War "—where the gamekeeper was lying in a drunken sleep—and were
hauling her along in a Ram Riding. There is
nothing so cruel as a crowd, and I have seen
nothing in my life like the face of These-an'-
That's wife. It was bleeding ; it was framed in

tangles of black, dishevelled hair; it was livid; but, above all, it was possessed with an awful fear—a horror it turned a man white to look on. Now and then she bit and fought like a cat: but the men around held her tight, and mostly had to drag her, her feet trailing, and the horns and kettles dinning in her wake.

There lay a rusty old ducking-cage among the lumber up at the town-hall; and some fellows had fetched this down, with the poles and chain, and planted it on the edge of the Town Quay, between the American Shooting Gallery and the World-Renowned Swing Boats. To this they dragged her, and strapped her fast.

There is no need to describe what followed. Even the virtuous women who stood and applauded would like to forget it, perhaps. At the third souse, the rusty pivot of the ducking-pole broke, and the cage, with the woman in it, plunged under water.

They dragged her ashore at the end of the pole in something less than a minute. They unstrapped and laid her gently down, and began to feel over her heart, to learn if it were still

beating. And then the crowd parted, and
These-an'-That came through it. His face wore
no more expression than usual, but his lips were
working in a queer way.

He went up to his wife, took off his hat, and
producing an old red handkerchief from the
crown, wiped away some froth and green weed
that hung about her mouth. Then he lifted her
limp hand, and patting the back of it gently,
turned on the crowd. His lips were still working. It was evident he was trying to say something.

"Naybours," the words came at last, in the
old dull tone; "I'd as lief you hadn' thought o'
this."

He paused for a moment, gulped down something in his throat, and went on—

"I wudn' say you didn' mean it for the best,
an' thankin' you kindly. But you didn' know
her. Roughness, if I may say, was never no
good wi' her. It must ha' been very hard for
her to die like this, axin your parden, for she
wasn' one to bear pain."

Another long pause.

" No, she cudn' bear pain. P'raps *he* might
ha' stood it better—though o' course you acted
for the best, an' thankin' you kindly. I'd as lief
take her home now, naybours, if 'tis all the same."

He lifted the body in his arms, and carried it
pretty steadily down the quay steps to his
market-boat, that was moored below. Two
minutes later he had pushed off and was
rowing it quietly homewards.

There is no more to say, except that the
woman recovered. She had fainted, I suppose,
as they pulled her out. Anyhow, These-an'-That
restored her to life—and she ran away the very
next week with the gamekeeper.

III —"DOUBLES" AND QUITS.

HERE is a story from Troy, containing two ghosts and a moral. I found it, only last week, in front of a hump-backed cottage that the masons are pulling down to make room for the new Bank. Simon Hancock, the outgoing tenant, had fetched an empty cider-cask, and set it down on the opposite side of the road; and from this Spartan seat watched the work of demolition for three days, without exhaustion and without emotion. In the interval between two avalanches of dusty masonry, he spoke to this effect:—

Once upon a time the cottage was inhabited by a man and his wife. The man was noticeable for the extreme length of his upper lip and gloom of his religious opinions. He had been a mate in the coasting trade, but settled down, soon after his marriage, and earned his living as one of the four pilots in the port. The woman

was unlovely, with a hard eye and a temper as
stubborn as one of St. Nicholas's horns. How
she had picked up with a man was a mystery,
until you looked at *him.*

After six years of wedlock they quarrelled
one day, about nothing at all: at least, Simon
Hancock, though unable to state the exact
cause of strife, felt himself ready to swear it was
nothing more serious than the cooking of the
day's dinner. From that date, however, the
pair lived in the house together and never
spoke. The man happened to be of the home-
keeping sort—possessed no friends and never
put foot inside a public-house. Through the
long evenings he would sit beside his own
fender, with his wife facing him, and never a
word flung across the space between them, only
now and then a look of cold hate. The few that
saw them thus said it was like looking on a pair
of ugly statues. And this lasted for four
years.

Of course the matter came to their minister's
ears—he was a "Brianite"—and the minister
spoke to them after prayer-meeting, one Wed-

nesday night, and called at the cottage early
next morning, to reconcile them. He stayed
fifteen minutes and came away, down the street,
with a look on his face such as Moses might
have worn on his way down from Mount Sinai,
if only Moses had seen the devil there, instead
of God.

At the end of four years, the neighbours remarked that for two days no smoke had issued
from the chimney of this cottage, nor had anyone seen the front door opened. There grew a
surmise that the quarrel had flared out at last,
and the wedded pair were lying within, in their
blood. The anticipated excitement of finding
the bodies was qualified, however, by a very
present sense of the manner in which the bodies
had resented intrusion during life. It was not
until sunset on the second day that the con-
stable took heart to break in the door.

There were no corpses. The kitchen was
tidy, the hearth swept, and the house empty.
On the table lay a folded note, addressed, in the
man's handwriting, to the minister.

" *Dear Friend in Grace,*" it began, " *we have
been married ten years, and neither has broken
the other; until which happens, it must be hell
between us. We see no way out but to part for
ten years more, going our paths without news of
each other. When that time's up, we promise
to meet here, by our door, on the morning of
the first Monday in October month, and try
again. And to this we set our names.*"—here
the two names followed.

. They must have set out by night; for an ex-
tinguished candle stood by the letter, with ink-
pot and pen.   Probably they had parted just
outside the house, the one going inland up the
hill, the other down the street towards the harbour.   Nothing more was heard of them.   Their
furniture went to pay the quarter's rent due to
the Squire, and the cottage, six months later,
passed into the occupation of Simon Hancock,
waterman.

At this point Simon shall take up the narra-
tive :—

" I'd   been   tenant   over   there "—with   a   nod

towards the ruin—"nine year an' goin' on for
the tenth, when, on a Monday mornin', about
this time o' year, I gets out o' bed at five o'clock
an' down to the quay to have a look at my boat;
for 'twas the fag-end of the Equinox, and ther'd
been a 'nation gale blowin' all Sunday and all
Sunday night, an' I thought she might have
broke loose from her moorin's.

"The street was dark as your hat and the
wind comin' up it like gas in a pipe, with a
brave deal o' rain.   But down 'pon the quay
day was breakin'—a sort of blind man's holiday,
but enough to see the boat by; and there she
held all right.   You know there's two postes
'pon the town-quay, and another slap opposite
the door o' the 'Fifteen Balls'?   Well, just
as I turned back home-long, I see a man
leanin' against thicky post like as if he was
thinkin', wi' his back to me and his front to the
'Fifteen Balls' (that was shut, o' course, at that
hour).   I must ha' passed within a yard of en,
an' couldn' figure it up how I'd a-missed seein'
en.   Hows'ever, 'Good-mornin'!' I calls out, in
my well-known hearty manner.   But he didn'

speak nor turn. 'Mornin'!' I says again. 'Can 'ee tell me what time 'tis? for my watch is stopped'—which was a lie; but you must lie now and then, to be properly sociable.

"Well, he didn' answer; so I went on to say that the 'Fifteen Balls' wudn' be open for another dree hour; and then I walked slap up to en, and says what the Wicked Man said to the black pig. 'You'm a queer Christian,' I says, 'not to speak. What's your name at all? And let's see your ugly face.'

"With that he turned his face; an' by the man! I wished mysel' further. 'Twas a great white face, all parboiled, like a woman's hands on washin' day. An' there was bits o' sticks an' chips o' sea-weed stuck in his whiskers, and a crust o' salt i' the chinks of his mouth; an' his eyes, too, glarin' abroad from great rims o' salt.

"Off I sheered, not azackly runnin', but walkin' pretty much like a Torpointer; an' sure 'nough the fellow stood up straight and began to follow close behind me. I heard the water go squish-squash in his shoon, every step he took. By this, I was fairly leakin' wi' sweat.

After a bit, hows'ever, at the corner o' Higman's store, he dropped off; an' lookin' back after twenty yards more, I saw him standin' there in the dismal grey light like a dog that can't make up his mind whether to follow or no. For 'twas near day now, an' his face plain at that distance. Fearin' he'd come on again, I pulled hot foot the few steps between me an' home. But when I came to the door, I went cold as a flounder.

"The fellow had got there afore me. There he was, standin' 'pon my door-step—wi' the same gashly stare on his face, and his lips a lead-colour in the light.

"The sweat boiled out o' me now. I quavered like a leaf, and my hat rose 'pon my head. 'For the Lord's sake, stand o' one side,' I prayed en; 'do'ee now, that's a dear!' But he wudn' budge; no, not though I said several holy words out of the Mornin' Service.

"'Drabbet it!' says I, 'let's try the back door. Why didn' I think 'pon that afore?' And around I runs.

"There 'pon the back door-step was a woman! —an' pretty well as gashly as the man. She was just a 'natomy of a woman, wi' the lines of her ribs showin' under the gown, an' a hot red spot 'pon either cheek-bone, where the skin was stretched tight as a drum. She looked not to ha' fed for a year; an', if you please, she'd a needle and strip o' calico in her hands, sewin' away all the while her eyes were glarin' down into mine.

"But there was a trick I minded in the way she worked her mouth, an' says I, 'Missus Polwarne, your husband's a-waitin' for 'ee, round by the front door.'

"'Aw, is he indeed?' she answers, holdin' her needle for a moment—an' her voice was all hollow, like as if she pumped it up from a fathom or two. 'Then, if he knows what's due to his wife, I'll trouble en to come round,' she says; 'for this here's the door *I* mean to go in by.'

But at this point Simon asserts very plausibly that he swooned off; so it is not known how they settled it.

[This story is true, as anyone who cares may assure himself by referring to Robert Hunt's "Drolls of the West of England," p. 357.]

IV.—THE BOY BY THE BEACH.

THERE are in this small history some gaps that can never be filled up; but as much as I know I will tell you.

The cottage where Kit lived until he was five years old stands at the head of a little beach of white shingle, just inside the harbour's mouth, so that all day long Kit could see the merchant-ships trailing in from sea, and passing up to the little town, or dropping down to the music of the capstan-song, and the calls and the creaking, as their crews hauled up the sails. Some came and went under bare poles in the wake of panting tugs; but those that carried canvas pleased Kit more. For a narrow coombe wound up behind the cottage, and down this coombe came not only the brook that splashed by the garden gate, but a small breeze, always blowing, so that you might count on seeing the white sails take it, and curve out

I

majestically as soon as ever they came opposite
the cottage, and hold it until under the lee of
the Battery Point.

Besides these delights, the cottage had a
plantation of ash and hazel above it, that
climbed straight to the smooth turf and the
four guns of the Battery; and a garden with a
tamarisk hedge, and a bed of white violets, the
earliest for miles around, and a fuchsia tree
three times as tall as Kit, and a pink climbing
rose that looked in at Kit's window and
blossomed till late in November. Here the
child lived alone with his mother. For there
was a vagueness of popular opinion respecting
Kit's father; while about his mother, unhappily,
there was no vagueness at all. She was a handsome, low-browed woman, with a loud laugh,
a defiant manner, and a dress of violent hues.
Decent wives clutched their skirts in passing
her: but, as a set-off, she was on excellent terms
with every sea-captain and mate that put into
the port.

All these captains and mates knew Kit and
made a pet of him: and indeed there was a

curious charm in the great serious eyes and reddish curls of this child whom other children shunned. No one can tell if he felt his isolation; but of course it drove him to return the men's friendship, and to wear a man's solemnity and habit of speech. The woman dressed him carefully, in glaring colours, out of her means: and as for his manners, they would no doubt have become false and absurd, as time went and knowledge came; but at the age of four they were those of a prince.

"My father was a ship's captain, too," he would tell a new acquaintance, "but he was drowned at sea—oh, a long while ago; years and years before I was born."

The beginning of this speech he had learned from his mother; and the misty antiquity of the loss his own childish imagination suggested. The captains, hearing it, would wink at each other, swallow down their grins, and gravely inform him of the sights he would see and the lands he would visit when the time came for him, too, to be a ship's captain. Often and often I have seen him perched, with his small

I 2

legs dangling, on one of the green posts on the
quay, and drinking in their talk of green ice-
bergs, and flaming parrots, and pig-tailed China-
men; of coral reefs of all marvellous colours,
and suns that burnt men black, and monkeys
that hung by their tails to the branches and
pelted the passers-by with coco-nuts; and the
rest of it. And the child would go back to the
cottage in a waking dream, treading bright
clouds of fancy, with perhaps a little carved
box or knick-knack in his hand, the gift of
some bearded, tender-hearted ruffian. It was
pitiful.

Of course he picked up their talk, and very
soon could swear with equal and appalling free-
dom in English, French, Swedish, German, and
Italian. But the words were words to him and
more, as he had no morals. Nice distinctions
between good and evil never entered the little
room where he slept to the sound only of the
waves that curved round Battery Point and
tumbled on the beach below. And I know
that, one summer evening, when the scandalised
townsmen and their wedded wives assembled,

and marched down to the cottage with intent to lead the woman in a " Ramriding," the sight of Kit playing in the garden, and his look of innocent delight as he ran in to call his mother out, took the courage out of them and sent them home, up the hill, like sheep.

Of course the truth must have come to him soon. But it never did: for when he was just five, the woman took a chill and died in a week.

She had left a little money; and the Vicar, rather than let Kit go to the workhouse, spent it to buy the child admission to an Orphanage in the Midlands, a hundred miles away.

So Kit hung the rose-tree with little scraps of crape, and was put, dazed and white, into a train and whisked a hundred miles off. And everybody forgot him.

Kit spent two years at the Orphanage in an antique, preposterous suit—snuff-coloured coat with lappels, canary waistcoat, and corduroy small-clothes. And they gave him his meals regularly. There were ninety-nine other boys who all throve on the food: but Kit pined.

And the ninety-nine, being full of food, made a racket at times; but Kit found it quiet—deathly quiet; and his eyes wore a listening look.

For the truth was, he missed the noise of the beach, and was listening for it. And deep down in his small heart the sea was piping and calling to him. And the world had grown dumb; and he yearned always: until they had to get him a new canary waistcoat, for the old one had grown too big.

At night, from his dormitory window, he could see a rosy light in the sky. At first he thought this must be a pillar of fire put there to guide him home; but it was only the glare of furnaces in a manufacturing town, not far away. When he found this out his heart came near to break; and afterwards he pined still faster.

One evening a lecture was given in the dining-room of the Orphanage. The subject was "The Holy Land," and the lecturer illustrated it with views from the magic-lantern.

Kit, who sat in one of the back rows, was

moderately excited at first. But the views of barren hills, and sands, and ruins, and palm-trees, and cedars, wearied him after a while. He had closed his eyes, and the lecturer's voice became a sing-song in which his heart searched, as it always searched, for the music of the beach; when, by way of variety—for it had little to do with the subject—the lecturer slipped in a slide that was supposed to depict an incident on the homeward voyage—a squall in the Mediterranean.

It was a stirring picture, with an inky sky, and the squall bursting from it, and driving a small ship heeling over white crested waves. Of course the boys drew their breath.

And then something like a strangling sob broke out on the stillness, frightening the lecturer; and a shrill cry—

"Don't go—oh, *damn it all!* don't go! Take me—take me home!"

And there at the back of the room a small boy stood up on his form, and stretched out both hands to the painted ship, and shrieked and panted.

There was a blank silence, and then the matron hurried up, took him firmly in her arms, and carried him out.

"Don't go—oh, for the Lord A'mighty's sake, don't go ! "

And as he was borne down the passages his cry sounded among the audience like the wail of a little lost soul.

The matron carried Kit to the sick-room and put him to bed. After quieting the child a bit she left him, taking away the candle. Now the sick-room was on the ground floor, and Kit lay still a very short while. Then he got out of bed, groped for his clothes, managed to dress himself, and, opening the window, escaped on to the quiet lawn. Then he turned his face south-west, towards home and the sea—and ran.

How could he tell where they lay ? God knows. Ask the swallow how she can tell, when in autumn the warm south is a fire in her brain. I believe that the sea's breath was in the face of this child of seven, and its scent in his nostrils, and its voice in his ears, calling, summoning all the way. I only know that he ran straight towards his home, a hundred miles off, and that next morning they found his canary waistcoat and snuff-coloured coat in a ditch, two miles from the Orphanage, due south-west.

Of his adventures on the road the story is equally silent, as I warned you. But the small figure comes into view again, a week later, on the hillside of the coombe above his home. And when he saw the sea and the white beach glittering beneath him, he did not stop, even for a moment, but reeled down the hill. The child was just a living skeleton; he had neither hat, coat, nor waistcoat; one foot only was shod, the other had worn through the stocking, and ugly red blisters showed on the sole as he ran. His face was far whiter than his shirt, save for a blue welt or two and some ugly red scratches; and his gaunt eyes were full of hunger and yearning, and his lips happily babbling the curses that the ships' captains had taught him.

He reeled down the hill to the cottage. The tenant was a newcomer to the town, and had lately been appointed musketry-instructor to

the battery above. He was in the garden prun-
ing the rose-tree, but did not particularly notice
the boy. And the boy passed without turning
his head.

The tide on the beach was far out and just
beginning to flow. There was the same dull
plash on the pebbles, the same twinkle as the
sun struck across the ripples. The sun was
sinking; in ten minutes it would be behind the
hill.

No one knows what the waves said to Kit.
But he flung himself among them with a chok-
ing cry, and drank the brine and tossed it over
his head, and shoulders and chest, and lay down
and let the small waves play over him, and cried
and laughed aloud till the sun went down.

Then he clambered on to a rock, some way
above them, and lay down to watch the water
rise; and watching it, fell asleep; and sleeping,
had his wish, and went out to the wide seas.

OLD ÆSON.

JUDGE between me and my guest, the stranger within my gates, the man whom in his extremity I clothed and fed.

I remember well the time of his coming, for it happened at the end of five days and nights during which the year passed from strength to age; in the interval between the swallow's departure and the redwing's coming; when the tortoise in my garden crept into his winter quarters, and the equinox was on us, with an east wind that parched the blood in the trees, so that their leaves for once knew no gradations of red and yellow, but turned at a stroke to brown, and crackled like tin-foil.

At five o'clock in the morning of the sixth day I looked out. The wind still whistled across the sky, but now without the obstruction of any cloud. Full in front of my window Sirius flashed with a whiteness that pierced the eye. A little to the right, the whole constellation of Orion was suspended clear over a wedge-like gap in the coast, wherein the sea could be guessed rather than seen. And, travelling yet further, the eye fell on two brilliant lights, the one set high above the other—the one steady and a fiery red, the other yellow and blazing intermittently—the one Aldebaran, the other revolving on the lighthouse top, fifteen miles away.

Half-way up the east, the moon, now in her last quarter and decrepit, climbed with the dawn close at her heels. And at this hour they brought in the Stranger, asking if my pleasure were to give him clothing and hospitality.

Nobody knew whence he came—except that it was from the wind and the night—seeing that he spoke in a strange tongue, moaning and making a sound like the twittering of birds in a chimney. But his journey must have been long and painful; for his legs bent under him, and he could not stand when they lifted him. So, finding it useless to question him for the time,

I learnt from the servants all they had to tell
—namely, that they had come upon him, but
a few minutes before, lying on his face within
my grounds, without staff or scrip, bareheaded,
spent, and crying feebly for succour in his
foreign tongue; and that in pity they had
carried him in and brought him to me.

Now for the look of this man, he seemed
a century old, being bald, extremely wrinkled,
with wide hollows where the teeth should be,
and the flesh hanging loose and flaccid on his
cheek-bones; and what colour he had could
have come only from exposure to that bitter
night. But his eyes chiefly spoke of his extreme age. They were blue and deep, and filled
with the wisdom of years; and when he turned
them in my direction they appeared to look
through me, beyond me, and back upon cen-
turies of sorrow and the slow endurance of
man, as if his immediate misfortune were but
an inconsiderable item in a long list. They
frightened me. Perhaps they conveyed a
warning of that which I was to endure at
their owner's hands. From compassion, I

ordered the servants to take him to my wife,
with word that I wished her to set food before
him, and see that it passed his lips.

So much I did for this Stranger. Now learn
how he rewarded me.

He has taken my youth from me, and the
most of my substance, and the love of my
wife.

From the hour when he tasted food in my
house, he sat there without hint of going.
Whether from design, or because age and his
sufferings had really palsied him, he came back
tediously to life and warmth, nor for many days
professed himself able to stand erect. Mean-
while he lived on the best of our hospitality.
My wife tended him, and my servants ran at his
bidding; for he managed early to make them
understand scraps of his language, though slow
in acquiring ours—I believe out of calculation,
lest someone should inquire his business (which
was a mystery) or hint at his departure. I
myself often visited the room he had appro-
priated, and would sit for an hour watching

those fathomless eyes while I tried to make head or tail of his discourse. When we were alone, my wife and I used to speculate at times on his probable profession. Was he a merchant? —an aged mariner?—a tinker, tailor, beggarman, thief? We could never decide, and he never disclosed.

Then the awakening came. I sat one day in the chair beside his, wondering as usual. I had felt heavy of late, with a soreness and languor in my bones, as if a dead weight hung continually on my shoulders, and another rested on my heart. A warmer colour in the Stranger's cheek caught my attention; and I bent forward, peering under the pendulous lids. His eyes were livelier and less profound. The melancholy was passing from them as breath fades off a pane of glass. *He was growing younger.* Starting up, I ran across the room, to the mirror.

There were two white hairs in my fore-lock; and, at the corner of either eye, half a dozen radiating lines. I was an old man.

Turning, I regarded the Stranger. He sat phlegmatic as an Indian idol; and in my fancy

I felt the young blood draining from my own heart, and saw it mantling in his cheeks. Minute by minute I watched the slow miracle— the old man beautified. As buds unfold, he put on a lovely youthfulness; and, drop by drop, left me winter.

I hurried from the room, and seeking my wife, laid the case before her. "This is a ghoul," I said, " that we harbour : he is sucking my best blood, and the household is clean bewitched." She laid aside the book in which she read, and laughed at me. Now my wife was well-looking, and her eyes were the light of my soul. Consider, then, how I felt as she laughed, taking the Stranger's part against me. When I left her, it was with a new suspicion in my heart. " How shall it be," I thought, "if after stealing my youth, he go on to take the one thing that is better ? "

In my room, day by day, I brooded upon this—hating my own alteration, and fearing worse. With the Stranger there was no longer any disguise. His head blossomed in curls; white teeth filled the hollows of his mouth ; the pits in his cheeks were heaped full with roses, glowing under a transparent skin. It was Æson renewed and thankless; and he sat on, devouring my substance.

Now having probed my weakness, and being satisfied that I no longer dared to turn him out, he, who had half-imposed his native tongue upon us, constraining the household to a hideous jargon, the bastard growth of two languages, condescended to jerk us back rudely into our own speech once more, mastering it with a readiness that proved his former dissimulation, and using it henceforward as the sole vehicle of his wishes. On his past life he remained silent; but took occasion to confide in me that he proposed embracing a military career, as soon as he should tire of the shelter of my roof.

And I groaned in my chamber; for that which I feared had come to pass. He was making open love to my wife. And the eyes with which he looked at her, and the lips with which he coaxed her, had been mine; and I was an old man. Judge now between me and this guest.

J

One morning I went to my wife; for the burden was past bearing, and I must satisfy myself. I found her tending the plants on her window-ledge; and when she turned, I saw that years had not taken from her comeliness one jot. And I was old.

So I taxed her on the matter of this Stranger, saying this and that, and how I had cause to believe he loved her.

" That is beyond doubt," she answered, and smiled.

" By my head, I believe his fancy is returned ! " I blurted out.

And her smile grew radiant, as, looking me in the face, she answered, " By my soul, husband, it is."

Then I went from her, down into my garden, where the day grew hot and the flowers were beginning to droop. I stared upon them and could find no solution to the problem that worked in my heart. And then I glanced up, eastward, to the sun above the privet-hedge, and saw *him* coming across the flower beds, treading them down in wantonness. He came with a light step and a smile, and I waited for him, leaning heavily on my stick.

"Give me your watch!" he called out, as he drew near.

"Why should I give you my watch?" I asked, while something worked in my throat.

"Because I wish it; because it is gold; because you are too old, and won't want it much longer."

"Take it," I cried, pulling the watch out and thrusting it into his hand. "Take it—you who have taken all that is better! Strip me, spoil me—— "

A soft laugh sounded above, and I turned. My wife was looking down on us from the window, and her eyes were both moist and glad.

"Pardon me," she said, "it is you who are spoiling the child."

STORIES OF BLEAKIRK.

I.—THE AFFAIR OF BLEAKIRK-ON-SANDS.

*[The events, which took place on November 23,
186–, are narrated by Reuben Cartwright,
Esq., of Bleakirk Hall, Bleakirk-on-Sands,
in the North Riding of Yorkshire.]*

A ROUGH, unfrequented bridle-road rising and
dipping towards the coast, with here and there
a glimpse of sea beyond the sad-coloured moors:
straight overhead, a red and wintry sun just
struggling to assert itself: to right and left, a
stretch of barren down still coated white with
hoar-frost.

I had flung the reins upon my horse's neck,
and was ambling homewards. Between me and
Bleakirk lay seven good miles, and we had
come far enough already on the chance of the
sun's breaking through; but as the morning
wore on, so our prospect of hunting that day
faded further from us. It was now high noon,
and I had left the hunt half an hour ago,

turned my face towards the coast, and lit a
cigar to beguile the way. When a man is
twenty-seven he begins to miss the fun of
shivering beside a frozen cover.

The road took a sudden plunge among the
spurs of two converging hills. As I began to
descend, the first gleam of sunshine burst from
the dull heaven and played over the hoar-frost.
I looked up, and saw, on the slope of the hill
to the right, a horseman also descending.

At first glance I took him for a brother
sportsman who, too, had abandoned hope of
a fox. But the second assured me of my
mistake. The stranger wore a black suit of
antique, clerical cut, a shovel hat, and gaiters;
his nag was the sorriest of ponies, with a
shaggy coat of flaring yellow, and so low in
the legs that the broad flaps of its rider's coat
all but trailed on the ground. A queerer turn-
out I shall never see again, though I live to be
a hundred.

He appeared not to notice me, but pricked
leisurably down the slope, and I soon saw that,
as our paths ran and at the pace we were going,

we should meet at the foot of the descent: which we presently did.

" Ah, indeed!" said the stranger, reining in his pony as though now for the first time aware of me : " I wish you a very good day, sir. We are well met."

He pulled off his hat with a fantastic politeness. For me, my astonishment grew as I regarded him more closely. A mass of lanky, white hair drooped on either side of a face pale, pinched, and extraordinarily wrinkled; the clothes that wrapped his diminutive body were threadbare, greasy, and patched in all directions. Fifty years' wear could not have worsened them; and, indeed, from the whole aspect of the man, you might guess him a century old, were it not for the nimbleness of his gestures and his eyes, which were grey, alert, and keen as needles.

I acknowledged his salutation as he ranged up beside me.

" Will my company, sir, offend you ? By your coat I suspect your trade : *venatorem sapit*—hey ?"

His voice exactly fitted his eyes. Both
were sharp and charged with expression; yet
both carried also a hint that their owner had
lived long in privacy. Somehow they lacked
touch.

" I am riding homewards," I answered.

" Hey ?   Where is that ? "

The familiarity lay rather in the words than
the manner; and I did not resent it.

" At Bleakirk."

His eyes had wandered for a moment to the
road ahead; but now he turned abruptly, and
looked at me, as I thought, with some suspicion.
He seemed about to speak, but restrained himself, fumbled in his waistcoat pocket, and producing a massive snuff-box, offered me a pinch.
On my declining, he helped himself copiously;
and then, letting the reins hang loose upon his
arm, fell to tapping the box.

" To me this form of the herb *nicotiana*
commends itself by its cheapness: the sense is
tickled, the purse consenting—like the com-
plaisant husband in Juvenal: you take me ?
I am well acquainted with Bleakirk-*super-*

sabulum. By the way, how is Squire Cartwright of the Hall ?"

"If," said I, "you mean my father, Angus
Cartwright, he is dead these twelve years."

"Hey ?" cried the old gentleman, and added
after a moment, "Ah, to be sure, time flies—
quo dives Tullus et—Angus, eh ? And yet a
hearty man, to all seeming. So you are his
son." He took another pinch. "It is very
sustaining," he said.

"The snuff ?"

"You have construed me, sir. Since I set
out, just thirteen hours since, it has been my
sole viaticum." As he spoke he put his hand
nervously to his forehead, and withdrew it.

"Then," thought I, "you must have started
in the middle of the night," for it was now little
past noon. But looking at his face, I saw
clearly that it was drawn and pinched with
fasting. Whereupon I remembered my flask
and sandwich-box, and pulling them out, assured him, with some apology for the offer,
that they were at his service. His joy was
childish. Again he whipped off his hat, and

clapping it to his heart, swore my conduct did
honour to my dead father; "and with Angus
Cartwright," said he, "kindness was intuitive.
Being a habit, it outran reflection; and his
whisky, sir, was undeniable. Come, I have a
fancy. Let us dismount, and, in heroic fashion,
spread our feast upon the turf; or, if the hoar-
frost deter you, see, here are boulders, and
a running brook to dilute our cups; and, by
my life, a foot-bridge, to the rail of which we
may tether our steeds."

Indeed, we had come to a hollow in the
road, across which a tiny beck, now swollen
with the rains, was chattering bravely. Falling
in with my companion's humour, I dismounted,
and, after his example, hitched my mare's rein
over the rail. There was a raciness about the
adventure that took my fancy. We chose two
boulders from a heap of lesser stones close beside
the beck, and divided the sandwiches, for though
I protested I was not hungry, the old gentleman
insisted on our sharing alike. And now, as
the liquor warmed his heart and the sunshine
smote upon his back, his eyes sparkled, and

he launched on a flood of the gayest talk—
yet always of a world that I felt was before
my time. Indeed, as he rattled on, the feeling
that this must be some Rip Van Winkle restored from a thirty years' sleep grew stronger
and stronger upon me. He spoke of Bleakirk,
and displayed a knowledge of it sufficiently
thorough—intimate even—yet of the old friends
for whom he inquired many names were unknown to me, many familiar only through their
epitaphs in the windy cemetery above the cliff.
Of the rest, the pretty girls he named were now
grandmothers, the young men long since bent
and rheumatic; the youngest well over fifty.
This, however, seemed to depress him little.
His eyes would sadden for a moment, then
laugh again. " Well, well," he said, " wrinkles,
bald heads, and the deafness of the tomb—we
have our day notwithstanding. Pluck the
bloom of it — hey? a commonplace of the
poets."

" But, sir," I put in as politely as I might,
" you have not yet told me with whom I have
the pleasure of lunching."

"Gently, young sir." He waved his hand towards the encircling moors. "We have feasted *more Homerico*, and in Homer, you remember the host allowed his guest fourteen days before asking that question. Permit me to delay the answer only till I have poured libation on the turf here. Ah! I perceive the whisky is exhausted: but water shall suffice. May I trouble you—my joints are stiff—to fill your drinking-cup from the brook at your feet?"

I took the cup from his hands and stooped over the water. As I did so, he leapt on me like a cat from behind. I felt a hideous blow on the nape of the neck: a jagged flame leapt up: the sunshine turned to blood—then to darkness. With hands spread out, I stumbled blindly forward and fell at full length into the beck.

When my senses returned, I became aware, first that I was lying, bound hand and foot and securely gagged, upon the turf; secondly, that the horses were still tethered, and standing quietly at the foot-bridge; and, thirdly, that my companion had resumed his position on

the boulder, and there sat watching my re-
covery.

Seeing my eyes open, he raised his hat and
addressed me in tones of grave punctilio.

"Believe me, sir, I am earnest in my regret
for this state of things. Nothing but the
severest necessity could have persuaded me to
knock the son of my late esteemed friend over
the skull and gag his utterance with a stone—
to pass over the fact that it fairly lays my sense
of your hospitality under suspicion. Upon my
word, sir, it places me in a cursedly equivocal
position!"

He took a pinch of snuff, absorbed it slowly,
and pursued.

"It was necessary, however. You will partly
grasp the situation when I tell you that my
name is Teague—the Reverend William Teague,
Doctor of Divinity, and formerly incumbent of
Bleakirk-on-Sands."

His words explained much, though not everything. The circumstances which led to the
Reverend William's departure from Bleakirk had
happened some two years before my birth: but

they were startling enough to supply talk in
that dull fishing village for many a long day.
In my nursery I had heard the tale that my
companion's name recalled : and if till now I
had felt humiliation, henceforth I felt absolute
fear, for I knew that I had to deal with a
madman.

"I perceive by your eyes, sir," he went on,
"that with a part of my story you are already
familiar : the rest I am about to tell you. It
will be within your knowledge that late on a
Sunday night, just twenty-nine years ago, my
wife left the Vicarage-house, Bleakirk, and never
returned ; that subsequent inquiry yielded no
trace of her flight, beyond the fact that she went
provided with a small hand-bag containing a
change of clothing ; that, as we had lived together for twenty years in the entirest harmony,
no reason could then, or afterwards, be given for
her astonishing conduct. Moreover, you will
be aware that its effect upon me was tragical ;
that my lively emotions underneath the shock
deepened into a settled gloom ; that my faculties
(notoriously eminent) in a short time became

clouded, nay, eclipsed—necessitating my re-
moval (I will not refine) to a madhouse. Hey,
is it not so ?"

I nodded assent as well as I could. He
paused, with a pinch between finger and thumb,
to nod back to me. Though his eyes were now
blazing with madness, his demeanour was for-
mally, even affectedly, polite.

" My wife never came back : naturally, sir—
for she was dead."

He shifted a little on the boulders, slipped the
snuff-box back into his waistcoat pocket, then
crossing his legs and clasping his hands over one
knee, bent forward and regarded me fixedly.

" I murdered her," he said slowly, and
nodded.

A pause followed that seemed to last an
hour. The stone which he had strapped in
my mouth with his bandanna was giving me
acute pain ; it obstructed, too, what little breathing my emotion left me ; and I dared not take
my eyes off his. The strain on my nerves grew
so tense that I felt myself fainting when his
voice recalled me.

K

" I wonder now," he asked, as if it were a riddle—" I wonder if you can guess why the body was never found ? "

Again there was an intolerable silence before he went on.

" Lydia was a dear creature : in many respects she made me an admirable wife.   Her affection for me was canine—positively.   But she was fat, sir ; her face a jelly, her shoulders mountainous. Moreover, her voice !—it was my cruciation— monotonously, regularly, desperately voluble.   If she talked of archangels, they became insignificant—and her themes, in ordinary, were of the pettiest.   Her waist, sir, and my arm had once been commensurate : now not three of Homer's heroes could embrace her.   Her voice could once touch my heart-strings into music; it brayed them now, between the millstones of the commonplace.   Figure to yourself a man of my sensibility condemned to live on these terms ! "

He paused, tightened his grasp on his knee, and pursued.

" You remember, sir, the story of the baker in Langius ?   He narrates that a certain woman

conceived a violent desire to bite the naked
shoulders of a baker who used to pass underneath her window with his wares. So impera-
tive did this longing become, that at length the
woman appealed to her husband, who (being a
good-natured man, and unwilling to disoblige
her) hired the baker, for a certain price, to come
and be bitten. The man allowed her two bites,
but denied a third, being unable to contain himself for pain. The author goes on to relate that,
for want of this third bite, she bore one dead
child, and two living. My own case," continued
the Reverend William, "was somewhat similar.
Lydia's unrelieved babble reacted upon her
bulk, and awoke in me an absorbing, fascinating
desire to strike her. I longed to see her quiver.
I fought against the feeling, stifled it, trod it
down : it awoke again. It filled my thoughts,
my dreams ; it gnawed me like a vulture. A
hundred times while she sat complacently turning her inane periods, I had to hug my fist to
my breast, lest it should leap out and strike her
senseless. Do I weary you ? Let me pro-
ceed :—

K 2

"That Sunday evening we sat, one on each side of the hearth, in the Vicarage drawing-room. She was talking—talking; and I sat tapping my foot and whispering to myself, 'You are too fat, Lydia, you are too fat.' Her talk ran on the two sermons I had preached that day, the dresses of the congregation, the expense of living, the parish ailments — inexhaustible, trivial, relentless. Suddenly she looked up and our eyes met. Her voice trailed off and dropped like a bird wounded in full flight. She stood up and took a step towards me. 'Is anything the matter, William?' she asked solicitously. 'You are too fat, my dear,' I answered, laughing, and struck her full in the face with my fist.

"She did not quiver much—not half enough —but dropped like a half-full sack on to the carpet. I caught up a candle and examined her. Her neck was dislocated. She was quite dead."

The madman skipped up from his boulder, and looked at me with indescribable cunning.

"I am so glad, sir," he said, "that you did not bleed when I struck you; it was a great

mercy. The sight of blood affects me—ah !"
he broke off with a subtle quiver and drew a
long breath. "Do you know the sands by
Woeful Ness—the Twin Brothers ?" he asked.

I knew that dreary headland well. For half
a mile beyond the grey Church and Vicarage of
Bleakirk it extends, forming the northern arm
of the small fishing-bay, and protecting it from
the full set of the tides. Towards its end it
breaks away sharply, and terminates in a dorsal
ridge of slate-coloured rock that runs out for
some two hundred feet between the sands we
call the Twin Brothers. Of these, that to the
south, and inside the bay, is motionless, and
bears the name of the 'Dead-Boy;' but the
'Quick-Boy,' to the north, shifts continually.
It is a quicksand, in short ; and will swallow a
man in three minutes.

"My mind," resumed my companion, "was
soon made up. There is no murder, thought I,
where there is no corpse. So I propped Lydia
in the armchair, where she seemed as if napping,
and went quietly upstairs. I packed a small
hand-bag carefully with such clothes as she

would need for a journey, descended with it, opened the front door, went out to be sure the servants had blown out their lights, returned, and hoisting my wife on my shoulder, with the bag in my left hand, softly closed the door and stepped out into the night. In the shed beside the garden-gate the gardener had left his wheel-barrow. I fetched it out, set Lydia on the top of it, and wheeled her off towards Woeful Ness. There was just the rim of a waning moon to light me, but I knew every inch of the way.

"For the greater part of it I had turf under-foot; but where this ended and the rock began, I had to leave the barrow behind. It was ticklish work, climbing down; for footing had to be found, and Lydia was a monstrous weight. Pah! how fat she was and clumsy—lolling this way and that! Besides, the bag hampered me. But I reached the foot at last, and after a short rest clambered out along the ridge as fast as I could. I was sick and tired of the business.

"Well, the rest was easy. Arrived at the furthest spit of rock, I tossed the bag from me

far into the northern sand. Then I turned to
Lydia, whom I had set down for the moment.
In the moonlight her lips were parted as though
she were still chattering; so I kissed her once,
because I had loved her, and dropped her body
over into the Quick-Boy Sand. In three
minutes or so I had seen the last of her.

"I trundled home the barrow, mixed myself
a glass of whisky, sat beside it for half an hour,
and then aroused the servants. I was cunning,
sir; and no one could trace my footprints on
the turf and rock of Woeful Ness. The missing
hand-bag, and the disarray I had been careful to
make in the bed-room, provided them at once
with a clue—but it did not lead them to the
Quick-Boy. For two days they searched; at
the end of that time it grew clear to them that
grief was turning my brain. Your father, sir,
was instant with his sympathy—at least ten
times a day I had much ado to keep from
laughing in his face. Finally two doctors
visited me, and I was taken to a madhouse.

"I have remained within its walls twenty-nine
years; but no—I have never been thoroughly at

home there. Two days ago I discovered that the place was *boring* me. So I determined to escape; and this to a man of my resources presented few difficulties. I borrowed this pony from a stable not many yards from the madhouse wall; he belongs, I think, to a chimney-sweep, and I trust that, after serving my purpose, he may find a way back to his master."

I suppose at this point he must have detected the question in my eyes, for he cried sharply,

"You wish to know my purpose? It is simple." He passed a thin hand over his forehead. "I have been shut up, as I say, for twenty-nine years, and I now discover that the madhouse bores me. If they re-take me—and the hue and cry must be out long before this—I shall be dragged back. What, then, is my proposal? I ride to Bleakirk and out along the summit of Woeful Ness. There I dismount, turn my pony loose, and, descending along the ridge, step into the sand that swallowed Lydia. Simple, is it not? *Excessi, evasi, evanui.* I shall be there before sunset—which reminds me," he added, pulling out his watch, "that my time is nearly up. I regret to leave you in this plight, but you see how I am placed. I felt, when I saw you, a sudden desire to unbosom myself of a secret which, until the past half-hour, I have shared with no man. I see by your eyes again that if set at liberty you would interfere with my purpose. It is unfortunate that scarcely a soul ever rides this way—I know the road of old. But to-morrow is Sunday: I will scribble a line and fix it on the church-door at Bleakirk, so that the parish may at least know your predicament before twenty-four hours are out. I must now be going. The bandanna about your mouth I entreat you to accept as a memento. With renewed apologies, sir, I wish you good-day ; and count it extremely fortunate that you did not bleed."

He nodded in the friendliest manner, turned on his heel, and walked quietly towards the bridge. As he untethered his pony, mounted, and ambled quietly off in the direction of the coast, I lay stupidly watching him. His black coat for some time lay, a diminishing blot, on

the brown of the moors, stood for a brief moment on the sky-line, and vanished.

I must have lain above an hour in this
absurd and painful position, wrestling with my
bonds, and speculating on my chances of passing
the night by the beck-side. My ankles were
tied with my own handkerchief, my wrists with
the thong of my own whip, and this especially
cut me. It was knotted immovably; but by
rolling over and rubbing my face into the turf,
I contrived at length to slip the gag down
below my chin. This done, I sat up and
shouted lustily.

For a long time there was no reply but the
whinnying of my mare, who seemed to guess
something was wrong, and pulled at her tether
until I thought she would break away. I think
I called a score of times before I heard an
answering "Whoo-oop!" far back on the road,
and a scarlet coat, then another, and finally a
dozen or more appeared on the crest of the
hill. It was the hunt returning.

They saw me at once, and galloped up,

speechless from sheer amazement. I believe
my hands were loosened before a word was
spoken. The situation was painfully ridiculous ;
but my story was partly out before they had
time to laugh, and the rest of it was gasped
to the accompaniment of pounding hoofs and
cracking whips.

Never did the Netherkirk Hunt ride after
fox as it rode after the Rev. William Teague
that afternoon. We streamed over the moor,
a thin red wave, like a rank of charging cavalry,
the whip even forgetting his tired hounds that
straggled aimlessly in our wake. On the hill
above Bleakirk we saw that the tide was out,
and our company divided without drawing rein,
some four horsemen descending to the beach,
to ride along the sands out under Woeful Ness,
and across the Dead-Boy, hoping to gain the
ridge before the madman and cut him off. The
rest, whom I led by a few yards, breasted the
height above and thundered past the grey
churchyard wall. Inside it I caught a flying
glimpse of the yellow pony quietly cropping
among the tombs. We had our prey, then,

enclosed in that peninsula as in a trap; but there was one outlet.

I remember looking down towards the village as we tore along, and seeing the fisher-folk run out at their doors and stand staring at the two bodies of horsemen thus rushing to the sea. The riders on the beach had a slight lead of us at first; but this they quickly lost as their horses began to be distressed in the heavy sand. I looked back for an instant. The others were close at my heels; and, behind again, the bewildered hounds followed, yelping mournfully. But neither man nor hound could see him whom they hunted, for the cliffs edge hid the quicksand in front.

Presently the turf ceased. Dismounting, I ran to the edge and plunged down the rocky face. I had descended about twenty feet, when I came to the spot where, by craning forward, I could catch sight of the spit of rock, and the Quick-Boy Sand to the right of it.

The sun—a blazing ball of red—was just now setting behind us, and its level rays fell full upon the man we were chasing.

He stood on the very edge of the rocks, a
black spot against the luminous yellow of
sea and sand. He seemed to be meditating.
His back was towards us, and he perceived
neither his pursuers above nor the heads that
at this moment appeared over the ridge behind
him, and not fifteen yards away. The party on
the beach had dismounted and were clambering
up stealthily. Five seconds more and they could
spring upon him.

But they under-estimated a madman's instinct. As if for no reason, he gave a quick
start, turned, and at the same instant was aware
of both attacking parties. A last gleam of sunlight fell on the snuff-box in his left hand;
his right thumb and fore-finger hung arrested,
grasping the pinch. For fully half a minute
nothing happened; hunters and hunted eyed
each other and waited. Then carrying the snuff
to his nose, and doffing his hat, with a satirical
sweep of the hand and a low bow, he turned
again and tripped off the ledge into the jaws
of the Quick-Boy.

There was no help now. At his third step

the sand had him by the ankles.   For a moment
he fought it, then, throwing up his arms, sank
forward, slowly and as if bowing yet, upon his
face.   Second by second we stood and watched
him disappear.   Within five minutes the ripples
of the Quick-Boy Sand met once more above
him.

In the course of the next afternoon the Vicar
of Bleakirk called at the Hall with a paper
which he had found pinned to the church door.
It was evidently a scrap torn from an old letter,
and bore, scribbled in pencil by a clerkly hand,
these words : "The young Squire Cartwright in
straits by the foot-bridge, six miles toward
Netherkirk.   *Orate pro anma Guliemli Teague.*"

II.—THE CONSTANT POST-BOY.

It was a stifling August afternoon. Not a breath of wind came over the downs, and the sky was just a great flaming oven inverted over them. I sat down under a dusty gorse-bush (no tree could be seen) beside the high-road, and tugging off a boot, searched for a prickle that somehow had got into it. Then, finding myself too hot to pull the boot on again, I turned out some crumbs of tobacco from a waistcoat pocket, lit my pipe, and unbuckled my pack.

I "travel" in Tracts, edifying magazines, and books on the Holy Land; but in Tracts especially. As Watteau painted the ladies and cavaliers of Versailles so admirably, because he despised them, so I will sell a Tract against any man alive. Also, if there be one kind of Tract that I loathe more than another, it is the Pink Tract. Paper of that colour is sacred to the Loves—to stolen kisses and assignations—and to see it with a comminatory text tacked on at

the foot of the page turns my stomach. I have
served in my time many different masters, and
mistresses; and it still pleases me, after quit-
ting their service, to recognise the distinction
between their dues. So it must have been the
heat that made me select a Pink Tract. I leant
back with my head in the shadow to digest its
crude absurdity.

It was entitled, "*How infernally Hot!*" I
doubt not the words were put in the mouth of
some sinner, and the moral dwelt on their literal
significance. But half-way down the first page
sleep must have descended on me : and I woke
up to the sound of light footsteps.

Pit-a-pat—pit-a-pat-a-pit-pat. I lifted my
head.

Two small children were coming along the
road towards me, hand-in-hand, through the
heat—a boy and a girl; who, drawing near and
spying my long legs sprawling out into the dust,
came to a stand, finger in mouth.

"Hullo, my dears!" I called out, "what are
you doing out in this weather ? "

The children stared at one another, and were

silent. The girl was about eight years old, wore a smart pink frock and sash, a big pink sun-bonnet, and carried an apple with a piece bitten out. She seemed a little lady; whereas the boy wore corduroys and a battered straw hat, and was a clod. Both children were exceedingly dusty and hot in the cheeks.

Finally, the girl disengaged her hand and stepped forward—

"If you please, sir, are you a clergyman?"

Now this confused me a good deal; for, to tell the truth, I had worn a white tie in my younger days, before. . . So I sat up and asked why she wished to know.

"Because we want to be married."

I drew a long breath, looked from her to the boy, and asked—

"Is that so?"

"She's wishful," answered he, nodding sulkily.

"Oho!" I thought; "Adam and Eve and the apple, complete. Do you love each other?" I asked.

"I adore Billy," cried the little maid "he's

L

the stable-boy at the 'Woolpack' in Blea-kirk——"

"So I am beginning to smell," I put in.

—"and we put up there last night—father and I. We travel in a chaise. And this morning in the stable I saw Billy for the first time, and to see him is to love. He is far below me in station,—ain't you, Billy dear? But he rides beautifully, and is ever so strong, and not so badly ed—educated as you would fancy: he can say all his 'five-times.' And he worships me,—don't you, Billy?"

"Washups," said Billy, stolidly.

"Do you mean to tell me you have trotted in this sun all the way from Bleakirk?" I inquired.

The girl nodded. She was a splendid child —dark-haired, proud of chin, and thoroughbred down to her very toes. And the looks of fondness she threw at that stable-urchin were as good as a play.

"And what will you do," I asked, "when you are married?"

"Go home and ask my father's forgiveness. He is proud; but very, very kind."

I told them I was a clergyman, and began to cast round in my mind what to do next; for the marriage service of the Church isn't exactly the thing to repeat to two babes, and the girl was quick enough to detect and resent any attempt at fooling. So at last I persuaded them to sit together under the gorse-bush, and told them that matrimony was a serious matter, and that a long exhortation was necessary. They settled themselves to listen.

      *   *   *   *   *

Having been twice married, I did not lack materials for a discourse. Indeed, when I talk of married life, it is a familiar experience with me to be carried away by my subject. Nor was I altogether surprised, on looking up after half an hour's oratory, to find the little ones curled in each other's arms, fast asleep.

So I spread my coat over them, and next (because the fancy took me, and not a breath of air was stirring) I treated them much as the robins treated the Babes in the Wood, strewing all my Tracts, pink and white, over them, till all

L 2

but their faces was covered. And then I set off
for the " Woolpack."

One spring morning, ten years later, I was
standing outside the " Woolpack," drinking my
mug of beer with a tall recruiting sergeant, and
discussing the similarity of our professions,
when a post-chaise appeared at the head of the
street, and a bobbing red postillion's jacket, and
a pair of greys that came down the hill with a
rattle, and drew up at the inn-door.

A young lady and a young gentleman sat in
the chaise, and the first glance told they were
newly married. They sat in the chaise, and
held each other by the hand, while the horses
were changing. And because I had a bundle of
tracts that fitted their condition, and because
the newly married often pay for a thing beyond
its worth, I approached the chaise-door.

The fresh horses were in as I began my
apologies ; and the post-boy was settling himself
in the saddle. Judge of my astonishment when
he leant back, cut me sharply across the calves
with his long whip, and before I could yell had

started his horses up the opposite hill at a gallop. The hind wheel missed my toes by an inch. In three minutes the carriage and red coat were but a speck on the road that led up to the downs.

I returned to my mug, emptied it moodily, broke a fine repartee on the sergeant's dull head (he was consumed with mirth), and followed the same road at a slow pace ; for my business took me along it.

I was on the downs, and had walked, perhaps, six miles, when again I saw the red speck ahead of me. It was the post-boy—a post-boy returning on foot, of all miracles. He came straight up to meet me, and then stood in the road, barring my path, and tapping his riding-boot with the butt of his whip—a handsome young fellow, well proportioned and well set up.

" I want you," he said, " to walk back with me to Bleakirk."

" Upon my word ! " I cried out. " Considering that Bleakirk is six miles away, that I am walking in the other direction, and that, two hours back, you gave me a cursed cut over the legs with that whip, I fancy I see myself obliging you!"

He regarded me moodily for about a minute, but did not shift his position.

"Why are you on foot?" I asked.

"Oh, my God!" he cried out quickly, as a man might that was stabbed; "I couldn't trust myself to ride; I *couldn't.*" He shuddered, and put a hand over his eyes. "Look here," he said, "you *must* walk home with me, or at least see me past the Chalk-pit."

Now the Chalk-pit, when spelt with a capital letter, is an especially deep and ugly one on the very edge of the Bleakirk road, about two miles out of the village. A weak fence only separates its lip from the macadam. It is a nasty place to pass by night with a carriage; but here it was broad day, and the fellow was walking. So I didn't take him at all.

"Listen to me," he went on in a dull voice; "do you remember sitting beside this road, close on ten years back? And a boy and girl who

came along this road together and asked you to
marry them ? "

" Bless my soul ! Were you that boy ? "

He nodded. " Yes: and the young lady in
the chaise to-day was that girl. Old man, I
know you reckon yourself clever,—I've heard
you talk: but that when I met her to-day,
three hours married, and she didn't know me, I
had a hell in my heart as I drove past the
Chalk-pit, is a thing that passes your understanding, perhaps. They were laughing together, mark you, and yet they weren't a hair's
breadth from death. And, by the Lord, you
must help me past that pit ! "

" Young man," I said, musing, " when first I
met you, you were ten years old, and I thought
you a fool. To-day you have grown into an
unmitigated ass. But you are dangerous;
and therefore I respect you, and will see you
home."

I turned back with him. When we came to
the Chalk-pit, I kept him on the farther side
of the road, though it cost me some terror to
walk between him and the edge; for I have

too much imagination to be a thoroughly brave man.

The sun was sinking as we walked down to Bleakirk; and the recruiting sergeant sat asleep outside the "Woolpack," with his head on the window-sill. I woke him up; and within half an hour my post-boy wore a bunch of ribbons on his cap—red, white, and blue.

I believe he has seen some fighting since then; and has risen in the ranks.

A DARK MIRROR.

In the room of one of my friends hangs a mirror. It is an oblong sheet of glass, set in a frame of dark, highly varnished wood, carved in the worst taste of the Regency period, and relieved with faded gilt. Glancing at it from a distance, you would guess the thing a relic from some "genteel" drawing-room of Miss Austen's time. But go nearer and look into the glass itself. By some malformation or mere freak of make, all the images it throws back are livid. Flood the room with sunshine; stand before this glass with youth and hot blood tingling on your cheeks; and the glass will give back neither sun nor colour; but your own face, blue and dead, and behind it a horror of inscrutable shadow.

Since I heard this mirror's history, I have stood more than once and twice before it, and peered into this shadow. And these are the simulacra I seem to have seen there darkly.

I have seen a bleak stone parsonage, hemmed in on two sides by a grave-yard ; and behind for many miles nothing but sombre moors climbing and stretching away. I have heard the winds moaning and wuthering night and morning, among the gravestones, and around the angles of the house ; and crossing the threshold, I know by instinct that this mirror will stand over the mantelpiece in the bare room to the left. I know also to whom those four suppressed voices will belong that greet me while yet my hand is on the latch. Four children are within—three girls and a boy —and they are disputing over a box of wooden soldiers. The eldest girl, a plain child with reddish-brown eyes, and the most wonderfully small hands, snatches up one of the wooden soldiers, crying, "This is the Duke of Welling-ton ! This shall be the Duke !" and her soldier is the gayest of all, and the tallest, and the most perfect in every part. The second girl makes her choice, and they call him "Gravey" because of the solemnity of his painted features. And then all laugh at the youngest girl, for she has

chosen a queer little warrior, much like herself;
but she smiles at their laughter, and smiles
again when they christen him "Waiting Boy."
Lastly the boy chooses. He is handsomer than
his sisters, and is their hope and pride; and has
a massive brow and a mouth well formed though
a trifle loose. His soldier shall be called Bona-
parte.

Though the door is closed between us, I can
see these motherless children under this same
blue mirror—the glass that had helped to pale
the blood on their mother's face after she left
the warm Cornish sea that was her home, and
came to settle and die in this bleak exile. Some
of her books are in the little bookcase here.
They were sent round from the West by sea,
and met with shipwreck. For the most part
they are Methodist Magazines—for, like most
Cornish folk, her parents were followers of
Wesley—and the stains of the salt water are
still on their pages.

I know also that the father will be sitting in
the room to my right—sitting at his solitary
meal, for his digestion is queer, and he prefers to

dine alone: a strange, small, purblind man, full
of sorrow and strong will. He is a clergyman,
but carries a revolver always in his pocket by
day, and by night sleeps with it under his
pillow. He has done so ever since some one
told him that the moors above were unsafe for
a person with his opinions.

All this the glass shows me, and more. I
see the children growing up. I see the girls
droop and pine in this dreary parsonage, where
the winds nip, and the miasma from the churchyard chokes them. I see the handsome promis-
ing boy going to the devil—slowly at first,
then by strides. As their hope fades from his
sisters' faces, he drinks and takes to opium-eat-
ing—and worse. He comes home from a short
absence, wrecked in body and soul. After this
there is no rest in the house. He sleeps in the
room with that small, persistent father of his,
and often there are sounds of horrible strug-
glings within it. And the girls lie awake, sick
with fear, listening, till their ears grow heavy
and dull, for the report of their father's pistol.
At morning, the drunkard will stagger out, and

look perhaps into this glass, that gives him back more than all his despair. " The poor old man and I have had a terrible night of it," he stammers; " he does his best—the poor old man ! but it's all over with me."

I see him go headlong at last and meet his end in the room above after twenty minutes' struggle, with a curious desire at the last to play the man and face his death standing. I see the second sister fight with a swiftly wasting disease; and, because she is a solitary Titanic spirit, refuse all help and solace. She gets up one morning, insists on dressing herself, and dies; and the youngest sister follows her but more slowly and tranquilly, as beseems her gentler nature.

Two only are left now—the queer father and the eldest of the four children, the reddish-eyed girl with the small hands, the girl who " never talked hopefully." Fame has come to her and to her dead sisters. For looking from childhood into this livid glass that reflected their world, they have peopled it with strange spirits. Men and women in the real world recognise the awful power of these spirits, without understanding them, not having been brought up themselves in front of this mirror. But the survivor knows the mirror too well.

" *Mademoiselle, vous êtes triste.*"

" *Monsieur, j'en ai bien le droit.*"

With a last look I see into the small, commonplace church that lies just below the parsonage : and on a tablet by the altar I read a list of many names. . .

And the last is that of Charlotte Brontë.

THE SMALL PEOPLE.

To a Lady who had asked
for a Fairy Tale.

You thought it natural, my dear lady, to lay this command on me at the dance last night. We had parted, two months ago, in London, and we met, unexpectedly and to music, in this corner of the land where (they say) the piskies still keep. And certainly, when I led you out upon the balcony (that you might not see the new moon through glass and lose a lucky month), it was not hard to picture the Small People at their play on the turf and among the dim flower-beds below us. But, as a matter of fact, they are dead, these Small People. They were the long-lived but not immortal spirits of the folk who inhabited Cornwall many thousands of years back—far beyond Christ's birth. They were "poor innocents," not good enough for heaven yet too good for the eternal fires; and when they first came, were of ordinary stature. But after Christ's birth they began to grow smaller and smaller, and at length turned into emmets and vanished from the earth.

The last I heard of them was a sad and serious little history, very different from the old legends. Part of it I was told by a hospital surgeon, of all people in the world. Part I learnt by looking at your beautiful gown last night, as you leant on the balcony-rail. You remember how heavy the dew was, and that I fetched a shawl for your shoulders. You did not wrap it so tightly round but that four marguerites in gold embroidery showed on the front of your bodice; and these come into the tale, the remainder of which I was taught this morning before breakfast, down among the cairns by the sea where the Small People's Gardens still remain—sheltered spots of green, with here and there some ferns and cliff-pinks left. For me they are libraries where sometimes I read for a whole summer's day; and with the help of the hospital surgeon, I bring you from them a story about your ball-gown which is perfectly true.

Twenty years ago — before the fairies had dwindled into ants, and when wayfarers were still used to turn their coats inside out, after nightfall, for fear of being " pisky-led "—there lived, down at the village, a girl who knew all the secrets of the Small People's Gardens. Where you and I discover sea-pinks only, and hear only the wash of the waves, she would go on midsummer nights and find flowers of every colour spread, and hundreds of little lights moving among them, and fountains and water-falls and swarms of small ladies and gentle-men, dressed in green and gold, walking and sporting among them, or reposing on the turf and telling stories to the most ravishing soft music. This was as much as she would relate; but it is certain that the piskies were friends of hers. For, in spite of her nightly wanderings, her housework was always well and cleanly done before other girls were dressed—the morning milk fresh in the dairy, the step sanded, the fire lit and the scalding-pans warming over it And as for her needlework, it was a wonder.

Some said she was a changeling; others that

M

she had found the four-leaved clover or the fairy
ointment, and rubbed her eyes with it.   But it
was her own secret; for whenever the people
tried to follow her to the " Gardens," *whir!
whir! whir!* buzzed in their ears, as if a flight
of bees were passing, and every limb would feel
as if stuck full of pins and pinched with
tweezers, and they were rolled over and over,
their tongues tied as if with cords, and at last,
as soon as they could manage, they would pick
themselves up, and hobble home for their
lives.

Well, the history—which, I must remind
you, is a true one—goes on to say that in time
the girl grew ambitious, or fell in love (I cannot
remember which), and went to London.   In any
case it must have been a strong call that took
her: for there are no fairies in London.   I regret
that my researches do not allow me to tell you
how the Small People at home took her departure; but we will suppose that it grieved
them deeply.   Nor can I say precisely how the
girl fared for many years.   I think her fortune
contained both joy and sorrow for a while; and

I suspect that many passages of her life would be sadly out of place in this story, even if they could be hunted out. Indeed, fairy-tales have to omit so much nowadays, and therefore seem so antiquated, that one marvels how they could ever have been in fashion.

But you may take it as sure that in the end this girl met with more sorrow than joy; for when next she comes into sight it is in London streets and she is in rags. Moreover, though she wears a flush on her cheeks, above the wrinkles it does not come of health or high spirits, but perhaps from the fact that in the twenty years' interval she has seen millions of men and women, but not one single fairy.

In those latter days I met her many times. She passed under your windows shortly before dawn on the night that you gave your dance, early in the season. You saw her, I think?— a woman who staggered a little, and had some words with the policeman at the corner : but, after all, a staggering woman in London is no such memorable sight. All day long she was seeking work, work, work ; and after dark she

M 2

sought forgetfulness. She found the one, in
small quantities, and out of it she managed to
buy the other, now and then, over the counter.
But she had long given up looking for the
fairies. The lights along the Embankment had
ceased to remind her of those in the Small
People's Gardens; nor did the noise bursting
from music-hall doors as she passed, recall the
old sounds; and as for the scents, there were
plenty in London, but none resembling that
of the garden which you might smell a mile
out at sea.

I told you that her needlework had been a
marvel when she lived down at the village.
Curiously enough, this was the one gift of the
fairies that stayed by her, and it remained as
wonderful as ever. Her most frequent employer
was a flat-footed Jew with a large, fleshy face;
and because she had a name for honesty, she
was not seldom entrusted with costly pieces of
stuff, and allowed to carry them home to turn
into ball-dresses under the roof through the
gaps of which, as she stitched, she could see
the night pass from purple to black, and from

black to the lilac of daybreak. There, with a hundred pounds' worth of silk and lace on her knee, she would sit and work a dozen hours to earn as many pence. With fingers weary and—— But you know Hood's song, and no doubt have taken it to heart a dozen times.

It came to this, however, that one evening, when she had not eaten for forty hours, her employer gave her a piece of embroidery to work against time. The fact is, my dear lady, that you are very particular about having your commissions executed to the hour, and your dressmakers are anxious to oblige, knowing that you never squabble over the price. To be sure, you have never heard of the flat-footed Jew man—how should you ? And we may believe that your dressmakers knew just as little of the poor woman who had used to be the friend of the Small People. But the truth remains that, in the press of your many pleasures, you were pardonably twenty-four hours late in ordering the gown in which you were to appear an angel.

Ah, madam ! will it comfort you to hear that

you were the one to reconcile the Small People with that poor sister of yours who had left them, twenty years before, and wanted them so sorely? The hospital doctor gave her complaint a long name, and I gather that it has a place by itself in books of pathology. But the woman's tale was that, after she had been stitching through the long night, the dawn came through the roof and found her with four marguerites still left to be embroidered in gold on the pieces of satin that lay in her lap. She threaded her needle afresh, rubbed her weary eyes, and began— when, lo! a miracle.

Instead of one hand, there were four at work—four hands, four needles, four lines of thread. *The four marguerites were all being embroidered at the same time!* The piskies had forgiven, had remembered her at last, after these many years, and were coming to her help, as of old. Ah, madam, the tears of thankfulness that ran from her hot eyes and fell upon those golden marguerites of yours!

Of course her eyes were disordered. There

was only one flower, really. There was only
one embroidered in the morning, when they
found her sobbing, with your bodice still in her
lap, and took her to the hospital; and that is
why the dressmakers failed to keep faith with
you for once, and made you so angry.

Dear lady, the piskies are not easily sum-
moned, in these days.

THE MAYOR OF GANTICK.

ONE of these days I hope to write a treatise on the Mayors of Cornwall—dignitaries whose pleasant fame is now night, remembered only in some neat by-word or saying of the country people. Thus you may hear, now and again, of "the Mayor of Falmouth, who thanked God when the town gaol was enlarged," "the Mayor of Market Jew, sitting in his own light," or "the Mayor of Calenich, who walked two miles to ride one." But the one whose history perplexed me most, till I heard the truth from an eye-witness, was "the mad Mayor of Gantick, whc was wise for a long day, and then died of it."

It was an old tin-streamer who told me—a thin fellow with a shrivelled mouth, and a back bent two-double. And I heard it on the very hearthstone of the Mayor's cottage, one afternoon, as we sat and smoked in the shadow of the crumbling mud wall, with a square of blue sky for roof, and for carpet a tangle of brambles, nettles, and rank grass.

It seems that the village of Gantick, half a mile away, was used once in every year to purge itself of evil. To this end the villagers prepared a huge dragon of pasteboard and marched out with it to a sandy common, since cut up by tin-works, but still known as Dragon's Moor. Here they would choose one of their number to be Mayor, and submit to him all questions of con-science, and such cases of notorious evil living as the law failed to provide for. Summary justice waited on all his decisions ; and as the village wag was usually chosen for the post, you may guess that the horse-play was rough at times. When this was over, and the public conscience purified, the company fell on the pasteboard dragon with sticks and whacked him into small pieces, which they buried in a small hollow called Dragon Pit ; and so returned gladly to their homes to start on another twelve months of sin.

This feast of purification fell always on the

12th of July; and in the heyday of its celebration there lived in this cottage a widow-woman and her only son, a demented man about forty years old. There was no harm in the poor creature, who worked at the Lanihorne slate-quarries, six miles off, as a "hollibubber"—that is to say, in carting away the refuse slate. Every morning he walked to his work, mumbling to himself as he went; and though the children followed him at times, hooting and flinging stones, they grew tired at last, finding that he never resented it. His mother—a tall, silent woman with an inscrutable face—had supper ready for him when he returned, and often was forced to feed him, while he unlocked his tongue and babbled over the small adventures of the day. He was not one of those gifted idiots who hear voices in the wind and know the language of the wild birds. His talk was merely imbecile; and, for the rest, he had large grey eyes, features of that regularity which we call Greek, and stood six foot two in his shoes.

One hot morning—it was the 12th of July—

he was starting for his work when an indescribable hubbub sounded up the road, and presently
came by the whole rabble of Gantick with cow-
horns and instruments of percussion, and in
their midst the famous dragon—all green, with
fiery, painted eyes, and a long tongue of red
flannel. Behind it the prisoners were escorted
—a pale woman or two with dazed, terrified
eyes, an old man suspected of egg-stealing, a
cow addicted to trespass, and so on.

The Mayor was not chosen yet, this ceremony being deferred by rule till the crowd
reached Dragon's Moor. But drawing near the
cottage door and catching sight of the half-
witted man with his foot on the threshold, a
village wit called out and proposed that they
should take "the Mounster" (as he was called)
along with them for Mayor.

It hit the mob's humour, and they cheered.
The Mounster's mother, standing in the doorway, went white as if painted.

"Man in the lump's a hateful animal," she
said to herself, hoarsely.   "Come indoors,
Jonathan, an' let 'em go by."

"Come an' rule over us," the crowd invited him, and a gleam of proud delight woke in his silly face.

"The heat—his head won't stand it." The woman looked up at the cloudless sky. "For God's sake take your fun elsewhere!" she cried.

The women who were led to judgment looked at her stupidly. They too suffered, without understanding, the heavy sport of men. At last one said—

"Old woman, let him come. We'll have more mercy from a mazed man."

"Sister, you've been loose, they tell me," answered the old woman, "an' must eat the bitter fruit o't. But my son's an innocent. Jonathan, they'll look for you at the works."

"There's prouder work for me 'pon Dragon's Moor," the Mounster decided, with smiling eyes. "Come along, mother, an' see me exalted."

The crowd bore him off at their head, and the din broke out again. The new Mayor strutted among them with lifted chin and a radiant face. He thought it glorious. His

mother ran into the cottage, fetched a bottle
and followed after the dusty tail of the procession.   Once, as they were passing a running
stream, she halted and filled the bottle carefully, emptying it again and again until the
film outside the glass was to her liking.
Then she followed again, and came to Dragon's
Moor.

They sat the Mayor on a mound, took off his
hat, placed a crown on his head and a broomstick in his hand, and brought him the cases to
try.

The first was a grey mare, possessed (they
alleged) with a devil. Her skin hung like a
sack on her bones.

"'Tis Eli Thoms' mare.   What's to be done
to cure her?" they asked.

"Let Eli Thoms buy a comb, an' comb his
mare's tail while she eats her feed. So Eli 'll
know if 'tis the devil or no that steals oats from
his manger."

They applauded his wisdom and brought
forward the woman who had pleaded just now
with his mother.

"Who made her?" he asked, having listened to the charge.

"God, 'tis to be supposed."

"God makes no evil."

"The Devil, then."

"Then whack the Devil."

They fell on the pasteboard dragon and belaboured him. The sun poured down on the Mayor's throne; and his mother, who sat by his right hand wondering at his sense, gave him water to drink from the bottle. They brought a third case—a boy who had been caught torturing a cow. He had taken a saw, and tried to saw off one of her horns while she was tethered in her stall.

The Mayor leapt up from his seat.

"Kill him!" he shouted, "take him off and kill him!" His face was twisted with passion, and he lifted his stick. The crowd fell back for a second, but the old woman leant forward and touched her son softly on the leg. He stopped short: the anger died out of his face, and he shivered.

"No," he said, "I was wrong, naybours. The

boy is mad, I think; an' 'tis a terrible lot, to be mad. This is the Devil's doing, out o' doubt. Beat the Devil."

"Simme," said one in the crowd, "the sins o' Gantick be wearin' out the smoky man at a terrible rate."

"Ay," answered another, "His Naughtiness bain't ekal to Gantick." And this observation was the original of a proverb, still repeated— "As naughty as Gantick, where the Devil struck for shorter hours."

There was no cruelty that day on Dragon's Moor. All the afternoon the mad Mayor sat in the sun's eye and gave judgment, while his mother from time to time wiped away the froth that gathered on his lips, and moistened them with water from her bottle. From first to last she never spoke a word, but sat with a horror in her eyes, and watched the flushed cheeks of this grown-up, bearded son. And all the afternoon the men of Gantick brayed the Devil into shreds.

I said there was no cruelty on Dragon's

Moor that day. But at sundown the Mayor turned to his mother and said—

" We've been over-hasty, mother. We ought to ha' found out who made the Devil what he is."

At last the sun dropped; a shadow fell on the brown moors and crept up the mound where the mother and son sat. The brightness died out of the Mayor's face.

Three minutes after, he flung up his hands and cried, " Mother—my head, my head!"

She rose, still without a word, pulled down his arms, slipped one within her own, and led him away to the road. The crowd did not interfere; they were burying the broken dragon, with shouts and rough play.

A woman followed them to the road, and tried to clasp the Mayor's knees as he staggered.

His mother beat her away.

"Off wi' you!" she cried; " 'tis your reproach he's bearin'."

She helped him slowly home. In the shadow of the cottage the inspired look that he had worn all day returned for a moment. Then a convulsion took him, casting him on the floor.

N

At nine o'clock he died, with his head on her lap.

She closed his eyes, smoothed the wrinkles on his tired face, and sat watching him for some time. At length she lifted and laid him on the deal table at full length, bolted the door, put the heavy shutter on the low window, and began to light the fire.

For fuel she had a heap of peat-turves and some sticks. Having lit it, she set a crock of water to warm, and undressed the man slowly. Then, the water being ready, she washed and laid him out, chafing his limbs and talking to herself all the while.

"Fair, straight legs," she said; "beautiful body that leapt in my side, forty years back, and thrilled me! How proud I was! Why did God make you beautiful?"

All night she sat caressing him. And the smoke of the peat-turves, finding no exit and no draught to carry them up the chimney, crept around and killed her quietly beside her son.

THE DOCTOR'S FOUNDLING.

THERE are said to be many vipers on the Downs above the sea; but it was so pleasant to find a breeze up there allaying the fervid afternoon, that I risked the consequences and stretched myself at full length, tilting my straw hat well over my nose.

Presently, above the *tic-a-tic-tick* of the grasshoppers, and the wail of a passing gull, a human sound seemed to start abruptly out of the solitude—the voice of a man singing. I rose on my elbow, and pushed the straw hat up a bit. Under its brim through the quivering atmosphere, I saw the fellow, two hundred yards away, a dark obtrusive blot on the bronze landscape. He was coming along the track that would lead him down-hill to the port; and his voice fell louder on the still air—

> " *Ho ! the prickly briar;*
>   *It prickles my throat so sore—*
>   *If I get out o' the prickly briar,*
>   *I'll never get in any more.*
>
>   *Ho ! just loosen the rope*"——

At this point I must have come within his view, for he halted a moment, and then turned abruptly out of the track towards me, —a scare-crow of a figure, powdered white with dust. In spite of the weather, he wore his tattered coat buttoned at the throat, with the collar turned up. Probably he possessed no shirt ; certainly no socks, for his toes protruded from the broken boots. He was quite young.

Without salutation he dropped on the turf two paces off and remarked—

" It's bleedin' 'ot."

There was just a pause while he cast his eyes back on the country he had travelled ; then, jerking his thumb over his shoulder in the direction of the port, he inquired—

" 'Ow's the old lot ? "

Said I, " Look here; you're Dick Jago. How far have you walked to-day ? "

He had turned on me as if ready with a sharp question, but changed his mind and answered doggedly—

" All the way from Drakeport."

" Very well; then it's right-about-face with you and back to Drakeport before I let you go. Do you see this stick ? If you attempt to walk a step more towards the port, I'll crack your head with it."

He gulped down something in his throat. " Is the old man ill ? " he asked.

" He's dead," said I, simply.

The fellow turned his eyes to the horizon, and began whistling the air of " The Prickly Briar " softly to himself. And while he whistled, my memory ran back to the day when he first came to trouble us, and play the fiend's mischief with a couple of dear honest hearts.

The day I travelled back to was one in the prime of May, when the lilacs were out by Dr. Jago's green gate, and the General from

Drakeport Barracks, with the red and white
feathers in his cocked-hat, had just cantered
up the street, followed by a dozen shouting
urchins, on his way to the Downs.   For it
was the end of the militia-training, when the
review was always held; and all the morning
the bugles had been sounding at the head
of every street and lane where the men were
billeted.

When the gold-laced General disappeared, he
left the streets all but empty; for the towns-
people by this time had flocked to the Downs.
Only by Dr. Jago's gate there stood a small
group in the sunshine.   Kitty, the doctor's mare
that had pulled his gig for ten years, was
standing saddled in the roadway, with a stable-
boy at her head; just outside the gate, the little
doctor himself in regimentals and black cocked-
hat with black feathers, regarding her; behind,
the pleasant old face of his wife, regarding *him* ;
and, behind again, the two maid-servants regarding the group generally from behind their
mistress's shoulder.

" Maria, I shall never do it," said the doctor,

measuring with his eye the distance between the ground and the stirrup.

"Indeed, John, I don't think you will."

"There was a time when I'd have vaulted it. I'm abominably late as it is, Maria."

"Shall I give master a leg up?" suggested one of the maids.

"No, Susan, you will do nothing of the kind." Mrs. Jago paused, her brow wrinkled beneath her white lace cap. Then an inspiration came—"The chair—a kitchen chair, Susan!"

The maid flew; the chair was brought; and that is how the good old doctor mounted for the review. Three minutes later he was trotting soberly up the street, pausing twice to kiss his hand to his wife, who watched him proudly from the green gate, and took off her spectacles and wiped them, the better to see him out of sight.

By the time Dr. Jago reached the Downs, the review was in full swing. The colonel shouted, the captains shouted, the regiment formed, re-formed, marched, charged at the double, and fired volleys of blank cartridges. The General and orderlies galloped from spot to spot without apparent object ; and all was very martial. At last the doctor grew tired of trotting up and down without being wanted. He thought with longing of some pools, half a mile away, in a hollow of the Downs, that contained certain freshwater shells about which he held a theory. The afternoon was hot. He glanced round—no one seemed to want him : so he turned Kitty into a grassy defile that led to the pools, and walked her leisurely away.

Half an hour later he stood, ankle-deep in water, groping for his shells and oblivious of the review, the firing that echoed far away, the flight of time—everything. Kitty, with one fore-leg through the bridle, was cropping on the brink. Minutes passed, and the doctor raised his head, for the blood was running into it. At that moment his eye was caught by a scarlet object under a gorse-bush on the opposite bank. He gave a second look, then waded across towards it.

It was a baby : a baby not a week old, wrapped only in a red handkerchief.

The doctor bent over it. The infant opened

its eyes and began to wail. At this instant an orderly appeared on the ridge above, scanning the country. He caught sight of the doctor and descended to the opposite shore of the pool, where he saluted and yelled his message. It appeared that some awkward militiaman had blown his thumb off in the blank cartridge practice and surgical help was wanted at once.

Doctor Jago dropped the corner of the handkerchief, returned across the pool, was helped on to Kitty's back and cantered away, the orderly after him.

In an hour's time, having put on a tourniquet and bandaged the hand, he was back again by the pool. The baby was still there. He lifted it and found a scrap of paper underneath. . . .

The doctor returned by devious ways to his home, a full hour before he was expected. He rode in at the back gate, where to his secret satisfaction he found no stable-boy. So he stabled Kitty himself, and crept into his own

house like a thief.   Nor was it like his habits to
pay, as he did, a visit to the little cupboard
(where the brandy-bottle was kept) underneath
the stairs, before entering the drawing-room,
with his face full of guilt and diplomacy.

"Gracious, John!" cried out Mrs. Jago,
dropping her knitting. "Is the review over
already?"

"No, I don't think it is—at least, I don't
know," stammered the doctor.

"John, you have had another attack of that
vertigo."

"Upon my honour I have not, Maria."   The
doctor was vehement; for the vertigo necessi-
tated brandy, and a visit to the little cupboard
below the stairs meant hideous detection.

So he sat up and tried to describe the review
to his wife, and made such an abject mess of it,
that after twenty minutes she made up her
mind that he *must* have a headache, and,
leaving the room quietly, went to the little cupboard below the stairs. She found the door
ajar. . . .

When, after a long absence, she reappeared

in the drawing-room, she had forgotten to bring the brandy, and wore a look as guilty as her husband's. So they sat together and talked in the twilight on trivial matters; and each had a heart insufferably burdened, and each was waiting desperately for an opportunity to lighten it.

"John," said Mrs. Jago at last, "we are getting poor company for each other."

"Maria!"

The doctor leapt to his feet: and these old souls, who knew each other so passing well, looked into each other's eyes, half in terror.

At that instant a feeble wail smote on their ears. It came from the cupboard underneath the stairs.

"Maria! I put it there myself, two hours ago. I picked it up on the downs. I've been——"

"*You!* I thought it was some beggar-woman's doing. John, John—why didn't you say so before!"

And she rushed out of the room.

This seedy scamp who reclined beside me was the child that she brought back with her from the little cupboard. They had adopted him, fed him, educated him, wrapped him round with love; and he had lived to break their hearts. Possibly there was some gipsy blood in him that defied their nurture. But the speculation is not worth going into. I only know that I felt the better that afternoon as I watched his figure diminishing on the road back to Drakeport. He had a crown of mine in his pocket, and was still singing—

> *" Ho ! just loosen the rope,*
> *If it's only just for a while ;*
> *I fancy I see my father coming*
> *Across from yonder stile."*

I had lied in telling him that the old doctor was dead. As a matter of fact he lay dying that afternoon. Half-way down the hill I saw the small figure of Jacobs, the sexton, turn in at the church-gate. He was going to toll the passing-bell.

THE GIFTS OF FEODOR HIMKOFF.

It is just six years ago that I first travelled the coast from Gorrans Haven to Zoze Point.

Since then I have visited it in fair weather and foul; and in time, perhaps, shall rival the coastguardsmen, who can walk it blindfold. But to this day it remains in my recollection the coast I trod, without companion, during four dark days in December. It was a rude introduction. The wind blew in my face, with scuds of cold rain; a leaden mist hung low on the left, and rolled slowly up Channel. Now and then it thinned enough to reveal a white zigzag of breakers in front, and a blur of land; or, far below, a cluster of dripping rocks, with the sea crawling between and lifting their weed. But for the most part I saw only the furze-bushes beside the path, each powdered with fine rain-drops, that in the aggregate resembled a coat of grey frieze, and the puffs of spray that shot up over the cliff's lip and drenched me.

Just beyond the Nare Head, where the path dipped steeply, a bright square disengaged itself from the mist as I passed, and, around it, the looming outline of a cottage, between the footpath and the sea. A habitation more desolate than this odd angle of the coast could hardly have been chosen; on the other hand, the glow of firelight within the kitchen window was almost an invitation. It seemed worth my while to ask for a drink of milk there, and find out what manner of folk were the inmates.

An old woman answered my knock. She was tall, with a slight stoop, and a tinge of yellow pervading her face, as if some of the complexion had run into her teeth and the whites of her eyes. A clean white cap, tied under the chin with tape, concealed all but the edge of her grey locks. She wore a violet turnover, a large wrapper, a brown stuff gown that hardly reached her ankles, and thick worsted stockings, but no shoes.

" A drink o' milk ? Why not a dish o' tea ? "

"That will be troubling you," said I, a bit

ashamed for feeling so little in want of sustenance.

"Few they be that troubles us, my dear. Too few by land, an' too many by sea, rest their dear souls! Step inside by the fire. There's only my old man here, an' you needn't stand 'pon ceremony wi' *he:* for he's stone-deaf an' totelin'. Isaac, you poor deaf haddock, here's a strange body for 'ee to look at; tho' you'm past all pomp but buryin', I reckon." She sighed as I stepped past into the warmth.

The man she called Isaac was huddled and nodding in a chair, before the bluish blaze of a wreck-wood fire. He met me with an incurious stare, and began to doze again. He was clearly in the last decline of manhood, the stage of utter childishness and mere oblivion; and sat there with his faculties collapsed, waiting for release.

My mired boots played havoc with the neatly sanded floor; but the old woman dusted a chair for me as carefully as if I had worn robes of state, and set it on the other side of the hearth. Then she put the kettle to boil, and unhitching a cup from the dresser, took a key from it, and opened a small cupboard between the fireplace and the wall. That which she sought stood on the top shelf, and she had to climb on a chair to reach it. I offered my help; but no—she would get it herself. It proved to be a small green canister.

The tea that came from this canister I wish I could describe. No sooner did the boiling water touch it than the room was filled with fragrance. The dotard in the chair drew a long breath through his nostrils, as though the aroma touched some quick centre in his moribund brain. The woman poured out a cup, and I sipped it.

"Smuggled," I thought to myself; for indeed you cannot get such tea in London if you pay fifty shillings a pound.

"You like it?" she asked. Before I could answer, a small table stood at my elbow, and she was loading it with delicacies from the cupboard. The contents of that cupboard! Caviare came from it, and a small ambrosial cheese; dried figs and guava jelly; olives, cherries in brandy, wonderful filberts glazed with sugar; biscuits and all manner of queer Russian sweets. I leant back with wide eyes.

" Feodor sends us these," said the old woman, bringing a dish of Cornish cream and a home-made loaf to give the feast a basis.

" Who's Feodor ? "

" Feodor Himkoff." She paused a moment, and added, " He's mate on a Russian vessel."

" A friend ? "

The question went unnoticed. " Is there any you fancy ? " she asked. " Some o't may be outlandish eatin'."

" Do *you* like these things ? " I looked from her to the caviare.

" I don't know. I never tried. We keeps 'em, my man an' I, for all poor come-by-chance folks that knocks."

" But these are dainties for rich men's tables."

" May be. I've never tasted—they'd stick in our ozels if we tried."

I wanted to ask a dozen questions, but thought it politer to accept this strange hospitality in silence. Glancing up presently,

o

however, I saw her eyes still fixed on me, and
laid down my knife.

"I can't help it," I said, "I want to know
about Feodor Himkoff."

"There's no secret," she answered. "Least-
ways, there *was* one, but either God has condemned or forgiven afore now. Look at my
man there; he's done all the repentin' he's likely
to do."

After a few seconds' hesitation she went on—

"I had a boy, you must know—oh! a straight
young man—that went for a soldier, an' was
killed at Inkerman by the Rooshians. Take
another look at his father here; you think 'en a
bundle o' frailties, I dessay. Well, when the
news was brought us, this poor old worm lifts
his fist up to the sun an' says, ' God do so to me
an' more also,' he says, ' if ever I falls across a
Rooshian!' An' 'God send me a Rooshian—
just one!' he says, meanin' that Rooshians don't
grow on brambles hereabouts. Now the boy was
our only flesh.

"Well, sir, nigh sixteen year' went by, an' we
two were sittin', one quakin' night, beside this

very fire, hearkenin' to the bedlam outside: for 'twas the big storm in 'Seventy, an' even indoors we must shout to make ourselves heard. About ten, as we was thinkin' to alley-couchey, there comes a bangin' on the door, an' Isaac gets up an' lets the bar down, singin' out, ' Who is it ? '

" There was a big young man 'twixt the door-posts, drippin' wet, wi' smears o' blood on his face, an' white teeth showin' when he talked. 'Twas a half-furrin talk, an' he spoke a bit faint too, but fairly grinned for joy to see our warm fire,—an' his teeth were white as pearl.

" ' Ah, sir,' he cried, ' you will help ? Our barque is ashore below—fifteen poor brothers ! You will send for help ?—you will aid ? '

" Then Isaac stepped back, and spoke very slow—' What nation ? ' he asked. ' She is Russ —we are all Russ ; sixteen poor brothers from Archangel,' said the young man, as soon as he took in the question. My man slewed round on his heel, and walked to the hearth here ; but the sailor stretched out his hands, an' I saw the middle finger of his right hand was gone. ' You will aid, eh ? Ah, yes, you will aid. They are

o 2

clingin'—*so*—fifteen poor brothers, and many
have wives.' But Isaac said, 'Thank Thee, God,'
and picked up a log from the hearth here.
'Take 'em this message,' said he, facin' round;
an', runnin' on the sailor, who was faint and
swayin', beat him forth wi' the burnin' stick, and
bolted the door upon him.

"After that we sat quiet, he an' I, all the
night through, never takin' our clothes off. An'
at daybreak Isaac walked down to the shore.
There was nothin' to see but two bodies, an' he
buried them an' waited for more. That evenin'
another came in, an' next day, two; an' so on for
a se'nnight. Ten bodies in all he picked up and
buried i' the meadow below. An' on the fourth
day he picked up a body wi' one finger missin',
under the Nare Head. 'Twas the young man he
had driven forth, who had wandered there an'
broke his neck. Isaac buried him too. An' that
was all, except two that the coastguard found an'
held an inquest over an' carr'd off to churchyard.

"So it befell; an' for five year' neither Isaac
nor me opened mouth 'pon it, not to each other

even. An' then, one noonday, a sailor knocks
at the door; an' goin' out, I seed he was a
furriner, wi' great white teeth showin' dro' his
beard. 'I be come to see Mister Isaac Lenine,'
he says, in his outlandish English. So I called
Isaac out; an' the stranger grips 'en by the hand
an' kisses 'en, sayin', 'Little father, take me to
their graves. My name is Feodor Himkoff, an'
my brother Dmitry was among the crew of the
Viatka. You would know his body, if you
buried it, for the second finger was gone from
his right hand. I myself—wretched one!—
chopped it by bad luck when we were boys, an'
played at wood cuttin' wi' our father's axe. I
have heard how they perished, far from aid, and
how you gave 'em burial in your own field : and
I pray to all the saints for you,' he says.

"So Isaac led 'en to the field and showed 'en
the grave that was staked off 'long wi' the rest.
God help my poor man! he was too big a coward
to speak. So the man stayed wi' us till sundown, an' kissed us 'pon both cheeks, an' went
his way, blessin' us. God forgi'e us—God forgi'e
us!

"An' ever since he's been breaking our heads dro' the post-office wi' such-like precious balms as these here." She broke off to settle Isaac more comfortably in his chair. " 'Tis all we can do to get rid of 'em on poor trampin' fellows same as yourself."

YORKSHIRE DICK.

"SEE here, you'd best *lose* the bitch—till to-morrow, anyway. She ain't the sight to please a strict man, like your dad, on the Sabbath day. What's more, she won't heal for a fortni't, not to deceive a Croolty-to-Animals Inspector at fifty yards; an' with any man but me she'll take a month."

My friend Yorkshire Dick said this, with that curious gypsy intonation that turns English into a foreign tongue if you forget the words and listen only to the voice. He was squatting in the sunshine, with his back against an oak sapling, a black cutty under his nose, and Meg, my small fox-terrier, between his thighs. In those days, being just fifteen, I had taken a sketch-book and put myself to school under Dick to learn the lore of Things As They Are: and, as part of the course, we had been the death of a badger that morning—Sunday morning.

It was one of those days in autumn when the dews linger in the shade till noon and the blackberry grows too watery for the *connoisseur*. On the ridge where we loafed, the short turf was dry enough, and the sun strong between the sparse saplings; but the paths that zigzagged down the thick coppice to right and left were soft to the foot, and streaked with the slimy tracks of snails. A fine blue mist filled the gulf on either hand, and beneath it mingled the voices of streams and of birds busy beside them. At the mouth of each valley a thicker column of blue smoke curled up like a feather—that to the left rising from the kitchen chimney of my father's cottage, that to the right from the encampment where Dick's *bouillon* was simmering above a wood fire.

Looking over Dick's shoulder along the ridge I could see, at a point where the two valleys climbed to the upland, a white-washed building, set alone, and backed by an undulating moorland dotted with clay-works. This was Ebenezer Chapel; and my father was its deacon. Its one bell had sounded down the ridge and tinkled in my ear from half-past ten to eleven that morning. Its pastor would walk back and eat roast duck and drink three-star brandy under my father's roof after service. Bell and pastor had spoken in vain, as far as I was concerned; but I knew that all they had to say would be rubbed in with my father's stirrup-leather before nightfall.

" 'Tis pretty sport," said Dick, " but it leaves traces."

Between us the thin red soil of the ridge was heaped in mounds, and its stain streaked our clothes and faces. On one of these mounds lay a spade and two picks, a pair of tongs, an old sack, dyed in its original service of holding sheep's reddle, and, on the sack, the carcase of our badger, its grey hairs messed with blood about the snout. This carcase was a matter of study not only to me, who had my sketch-book out, but to a couple of Dick's terriers tied up to a sapling close by—an ugly mongrel, half fox— half bull-terrier, and a Dandie Dinmont—who were straining to get at it. As for Dick, he never lifted his eyes, but went on handling Meg.

He had the gypsy's secret with animals, and the
poor little bitch hardly winced under his touch,
though her under-lip was torn away, and hung,
like a red rag, by half an inch of flesh.

We had dug and listened and dug again for
our badger, all the morning. Then Dick sent his
mongrel in at the hole, and the mongrel had
come forth like a projectile and sat down at a
distance, bewailing his lot. After him the
Dandie went in and sneaked out again with a
fore-paw bitten to the bone. And at last Meg
stepped in grimly, and stayed. For a time
there was dead silence, and then as we pressed
our ears against the turf and the violets, that
were just beginning their autumnal flowering, we
heard a scuffling underground and began to dig
down to it, till the sweat streamed into our eyes.
Now Dick's wife had helped us to bring up the
tools, and hung around to watch the sport—an
ugly, apathetic woman, with hair like a horse's
tail bound in a yellow rag, a man's hips, and a
skirt of old sacking. I think there was no love
lost between her and Dick, because she had

borne him no children. Anyway, while Dick
and I were busy, digging like niggers and listening like Indians—for Meg didn't bark, not being
trained to the work, and all we could hear was
a *thud, thud* now and then, and the hard breathing of the grapple—all of a sudden the old hag
spoke, for the first time that day—

"S'trewth, but I've gripped!"

Looking up, I saw her stretched along the
side of the turf, with her head resting on the
lip of the badger's hole and her right arm inside,
up to the arm-pit. Without speaking again, she
began to work her body back, like a snake, the
muscles swelling and sinking from shoulder to
flank in small waves. She had the strength of a
horse. Inch by inch she pulled back, while we
dug around the mouth of the hole, filling her
mouth and eyes with dirt, until her arm came to
light, then the tongs she held; and then Dick
spat out a mighty oath—

"It's the *dog* she's got!"

So it was. The woman had hold of Meg all
the time, and the game little brute had held on
to the badger. Also the badger had held *her*,

and when at last his hold slipped, she was a
gruesome sight.   She looked round, reproach-
fully, shook the earth out of her eyes and went
in again without a sound.   And Dick picked up
a clod and threw it in his wife's face, between the
eyes.   She cursed him, in a perfunctory way, and
walked off, down the wood, to look after her
stew.

But now, Meg having pinned her enemy
again, we soon dug them out: and I held the
sack while Dick took the badger by the tail and
dropped him in.   His teeth snapped, a bare two
inches from my left hand, as he fell.   After a
short rest, he was despatched.   The method
need not be described.   It was somewhat crude,
and in fact turned me not a little sick.

"One o'clock," Dick observed, glancing up
at the sun, and resuming his care of Meg.
"What're ye trying to do, youngster?"

"Trying to put on paper what a badger's like
when he's dead.   If only I had colours——"

"My son, there's a kind of man afflicted with
an itch to put all he sees on paper.   What's the

use ?   Fifty men might sit down and write what
the grey of a badger's like ; and they can't, because there's no words for it.   All they can say
is that 'tis badger's-grey—which means nought
to a man that hasn't seen one ; and a man that
has don't want to be told.   Same with your
pencils and paints.   Cast your head back and
look up—how deep can you see into the sky ? "

" Miles."

" Ay, and every mile shining to the eye.   I've
seen pictures in my time, but never one that
made a dab of paint look a mile deep.   Besides,
why draw a thing when you can lie on your back
and look up at it ? "

I was about to answer when Dick raised his
head, with a queer alertness in his eyes.   Then
he vented a long, low whistle, and went on bind-
ing up Meg's jaw.

Immediately after, there was a crackling of
boughs to the left and my father's head appeared
above the slope, with the red face of the pastor
behind it.   We were caught.

On the harangue that followed I have no
wish to dwell.   My father and the pastor pitched

it in by turns, while Dick went on with his surgery, his mouth pursed up for a soundless whistle. The prosecution had it all its own way, and I felt uncomfortably sure about the sentence.

But at last, to our amazement, Dick, having finished the bandaging, let Meg go and advanced. He picked up my sketch-book.

"Gentlemen both," said he, "I've been listening respectful to your talk about God and his wrath, and as a poor heathen I'd like to know your idea of him. Here's a pencil and paper. Will you be kind enough to draw God? that I may see what he's like."

The pastor's jaw dropped. My father went grey with rage. Dick stood a pace back, smiling; and the sun glanced on the gold rings in his ears.

"No, sirs. It ain't blasphemy. But I know you can't give me a notion that won't make him out to be a sort of man, pretty much like yourselves—two eyes, a nose, mouth, and beard perhaps. Now my wife says there's points about a woman that you don't reckon into your notion, and my dog says there's more in a tail than most men estimate——"

"You foul-tongued poacher——" broke out my father.

"Now you're mixing matters up," Dick interrupted, blandly; "I poach, and that's a crime. I've shown your boy to-day how men kill badgers, and maybe that's wrong. But look here, sir—I've taught him some things besides; the ways of birds and beasts, and their calls; how to tell the hour by sun and stars; how to know an ash from a beech, of a pitch-dark night, by the sound of the wind in their tops; what herbs will cure disease and where to seek them; why some birds hop and others run. Sirs, I come of an old race that has outlived books and pictures and meeting-houses: you belong to a new one and a cock-sure, and maybe you're right. Anyhow, you know precious little of this world, whatever you may of another."

He stopped, pushed a hand through his coarse black hair, and, as if suddenly tired, resumed the old, sidelong gypsy look that he had been straightening with an effort.

" Your boy'll believe what you tell him : he's got the strength in his blood. Take him home and don't beat him too hard."

He glanced at me with a light nod, untied his dogs, shouldered his tools, and slouched away down the path, to sleep under his accustomed tree that night and be off again, next day, travelling amongst men and watching them with his weary ironical smile.

THE CAROL.

I WAS fourteen that Christmas:—all Veryan parish knows the date of the famous " Black Winter," when the *Johann* brig came ashore on Kibberick beach, with a dozen foreigners frozen stiff and staring on her fore-top, and Lawyer Job, up at Ruan, lost all his lambs but two. There was neither rhyme nor wit in the season; and up to St. Thomas's eve, when it first started to freeze, the folk were thinking that summer meant to run straight into spring. I mind the ash being in leaf on Advent Sunday, and a crowd of martins skimming round the church windows during sermon-time. Each morning brought blue sky, warm mists, and a dew that hung on the brambles till ten o'clock. The frogs were spawning in the pools; primroses were out by scores, and monthly roses blooming still ; and Master shot a goat-sucker on the last day in November. All this puzzled the sheep, I suppose, and gave them a notion that their time,

P

too, was at hand. At any rate the lambs fell
early; and when they fell, it had turned to
perishing cold.

That Christmas-eve, while the singers were
up at the house and the fiddles going like mad,
it was a dismal time for two of us. Laban
Pascoe, the hind, spent his night in the upper
field where the sheep lay, while I spent mine in
the chall* looking after Dinah, our Alderney,
that had slipped her calf in the afternoon—
being promised the castling's skin for a Sunday
waistcoat, if I took care of the mother. Bating
the cold air that came under the door, I kept
pretty cosy, what with the straw-bands round my
legs and the warm breath of the cows: for we
kept five. There was no wind outside, but
moonlight and a still, frozen sky, like a sounding board: so that every note of the music
reached me, with the bleat of Laban's sheep far
up the hill, and the waves' wash on the beaches
below. Inside the chall the only sounds were
the slow chewing of the cows, the rattle of a
tethering-block, now and then, or a moan from

* Cow-house.

Dinah. Twice the uproar from the house coaxed me to the door to have a look at Laban's scarlet lantern moving above, and make sure that he was worse off than I. But mostly I lay still on my straw in the one empty stall staring into the foggy face of my own lantern, thinking of the waistcoat, and listening.

I was dozing, belike, when a light tap on the door made me start up, rubbing my eyes.

" Merry Christmas, Dick ! "

A little head, bright with tumbled curls, was thrust in, and a pair of round eyes stared round the chall, then back to me, and rested on my face.

" Merry Christmas, little mistress."

" Dick—if you tell, I'll never speak to you again. I only wanted to see if 'twas true."

She stepped inside the chall, shutting the door behind her. Under one arm she hugged a big boy-doll, dressed like a sailor—from the Christmas-tree, I guessed—and a bright tinsel star was pinned on the shoulder of her bodice. She had come across the cold town-place in her muslin frock, with no covering for her shoulders;

and the manner in which that frock was hitched
upon her made me stare.

"I got out of bed again and dressed myself,"
she explained. "Nurse is in the kitchen, dancing with the young man from Penare, who can't
afford to marry her for *ever* so long, father says.
I saw them twirling, as I slipped out——"

"You have done a wrong thing," said I:
"you might catch your death."

Her lip fell:—she was but five. "Dick, I
only wanted to see if 'twas true."

"What?" I asked, covering her shoulders
with the empty sack that had been my pillow.

"Why, that the cows pray on Christmas-eve.
Nurse says that at twelve o'clock to-night all the
cows in their stalls will be on their knees, if only
somebody is there to see. So, as it's near twelve
by the tall clock indoors, I've come to see," she
wound up.

"It's quig-nogs, I expect. I never heard of
it."

"Nurse says they kneel and make a cruel
moan, like any Christian folk. It's because
Christ was born in a stable, and so the cows

know all about it. Listen to Dinah! Dick, she's going to begin!"

But Dinah, having heaved her moan, merely shuddered and was still again.

"Just fancy, Dick," the little one went on, "it happened in a chall like ours!" She was quiet for a moment, her eyes fixed on the glossy rumps of the cows. Then, turning quickly—"I know about it, and I'll show you. Dick, you must be Saint Joseph, and I'll be the Virgin Mary. Wait a bit——"

Her quick fingers began to undress the sailor-doll and fold his clothes carefully. "I *meant* to christen him Robinson Crusoe," she explained, as she laid the small garments, one by one, on the straw; "but he can't be Robinson Crusoe till I've dressed him up again." The doll was stark naked now, with waxen face and shoulders, and bulging bags of sawdust for body and legs.

"Dick," she said, folding the doll in her arms and kissing it—"St. Joseph, I mean—the first thing we've got to do is to let people know he's born. Sing that carol I heard you trying over last week—the one that says 'Far and far I carry it.'"

So I sang, while she rocked the babe:—

> " ' *Naked boy, brown boy,*
> *In the snow deep,*
> *Piping, carolling*
> *Folks out of sleep ;*
> *Little shoes, thin shoes,*
> *Shoes so wet and worn '*—
> ' *But I bring the merry news*
> *—Christ is born !*
>
> *Rise, pretty mistress,*
> *In your smock of silk ;*
> *Give me for my good news*
> *Bread and new milk.*
> *Joy, joy in Jewry,*
> *This very morn !*
> *Far and far I carry it*
> *—Christ is born !* ' "

She heard me with a grave face to the end ; then pulling a handful of straw, spread it in the empty manger and laid the doll there. No, I forget ; one moment she held it close to her

breast and looked down on it. The God who
fashions children can tell where she learnt that
look, and why I remembered it ten years later,
when they let me look into the room where she
lay with another babe in her clay-cold arms.

"Count forty," she went on, using the very
words of Pretty Tommy, our parish clerk;
"count forty, and let fly with 'Now draw
around——'"

> "*Now draw around, good Christian men,*
>   *And rest you worship-ping—*"

We sang the carol softly together, she resting
one hand on the edge of the manger.

"Dick, ain't you proud of him? I don't see
the spiders beginning, though."

"The spiders?"

"Dick, you're very ig-norant. *Everybody*
knows that, when Christ was laid in a manger,
the spiders came and spun their webs over Him
and hid Him. That's why King Herod couldn't
find Him."

"There, now! We live and learn," said I.

"Well, now there's nothing to do but sit

down and wait for the wise men and the shepheıds."

It wıs a little while that she watched, being long over-tired. The warm air of the chall weighed on her eyelids; and, as they closed, her head sank on my shoulder. For ten minutes I sat, listening to her breathing. Dinah rose heavily from her bed and lay down again, with a long sigh; another cow woke up and rattled her rope a dozen times through its ring; up at the house the fiddling grew more furious; but the little maid slept on. At last I wrapped the sack closely round her, and lifting her in my arms, carried her out into the night. She was my master's daughter, and I had not the courage to kiss so much as her hair. Yet I had no envy for the dancers, then.

As we passed into the cold air she stirred.

"Did they come? And where are you carrying me?" Then, when I told her, "Dick, I will never speak to you again, if you don't carry me first to the gate of the upper field."

So I carried her to the gate, and sitting up in my arms she called twice,

"Laban—Laban!"

"What cheer—O?" the hind called back. His lantern was a spark on the hill-side, and he could not tell the voice at that distance.

"Have you seen him?"

"Wha-a-a-t?"

"The angel of the Lo-o-ord!"

"Wha-a-a-t?"

"I'm afraid we can't make him understand," she whispered. "Hush; don't shout!" For a moment, she seemed to consider; and then her shrill treble quavered out on the frosty air, my own deeper voice taking up the second line—

"*The first 'Nowell' the angel did say*
Was to certain poor shepherds, in fields as
they lay,
—In fields as they lay, a-tending their sheep,
On a cold winter's night that was so deep—
Nowell! Nowell!
Christ is born in Israel!"

Our voices followed our shadows across the gate and far up the field, where Laban's sheep lay dotted. What Laban thought of it I cannot tell: but to me it seemed, for the moment, that the shepherd among his ewes, the dancers within the house, the sea beneath us, and the stars in their courses overhead moved all to one tune,—the carol of two children on the hill-side.

THE PARADISE OF CHOICE.

IT was not as in certain toy houses that foretell the weather by means of a man-doll and a woman-doll—the man going in as the woman comes out, and *vice versâ*. In this case both man and woman stepped out, the man half a minute behind; so that the woman was almost at the street-corner while he hesitated just outside the door, blinking up at the sky, and then dropping his gaze along the pavement.

The sky was flattened by a fog that shut down on the roofs and chimneys like a tent-cloth, white and opaque. Now and then a yellowish wave rolled across it from eastward, and the cloth would be shaken. When this happened, the street was always filled with gloom, and the receding figure of the woman lost in it for a while.

The man thrust a hand into his trousers pocket, pulled out a penny, and after considering for a couple of seconds, spun it carelessly.

It fell in his palm, tail up; and he regarded it as a sailor might a compass. The trident in Britannia's hand pointed westward, down the street.

"West it is," he decided with a shrug, implying that all the four quarters were equally to his mind. He was pocketing the coin, when footsteps approached, and he lifted his head. It was the woman returning. She halted close to him with an undecided manner, and the pair eyed each other.

We may know them as Adam and Eve, for both were beginning a world that contained neither friends nor kin. Both had very white hands and very short hair. The man was tall and meagre, with a receding forehead and a sandy complexion that should have been freckled, but was not. He had a trick of half-closing his eyes when he looked at anything, not screwing them up as seamen do, but appearing rather to drop a film over them like the inner eyelid of a bird. The woman's eyes resembled a hare's, being brown and big, and set far back, so that she seemed at times to be looking right behind her. She wore a faded look, from her dust-coloured hair to her boots, which wanted blacking.

"It all seems so wide," she began; "so wide——"

"I'm going west," said the man, and started at a slow walk. Eve followed, a pace behind his heels, treading almost in his tracks. He went on, taking no notice of her.

"How long were you in there?" she asked, after a while.

"Ten year'." Adam spoke without looking back. "'Cumulated jobs, you know."

"I was only two. Blankets it was with me. They recommended me to mercy."

"You got it," Adam commented, with his eyes fastened ahead.

The fog followed them as they turned into a street full of traffic. Its frayed edge rose and sank, was parted and joined again—now descending to the first-storey windows and blotting out the cabmen and passengers on omnibus tops, now rolling up and over the parapets of the houses and the sky-signs. It was noticeable that

in the crowd that hustled along the pavement
Adam moved like a puppy not yet waywise, but
with lifted face, while Eve followed with her
head bent, seeing nothing but his heels. She
observed that his boots were hardly worn at all.

Three or four times, as they went along,
Adam would eye a shop window and turn in at
the door, while Eve waited. He returned from
different excursions with a twopenny loaf, a red
sausage, a pipe, box of lights and screw of
tobacco, and a noggin or so of gin in an old
soda-water bottle. Once they turned aside into
a public, and had a drink of gin together. Adam
paid.

Thus for two hours they plodded westward,
and the fog and crowd were with them all the
way—strangers jostling them by the shoulder
on the greasy pavement, hansoms splashing the
brown mud over them—the same din for miles.
Many shops were lighting up, and from these a
yellow flare streamed into the fog; or a white
when it came from the electric light ; or separate
beams of orange, green, and violet, when the
shop was a druggist's.

Then they came to the railings of Hyde
Park, and trudged down the hill alongside them
to Kensington Gardens.   It was yet early in the
afternoon.   Adam pulled up.

" Come and look," he said.   " It's autumn in
there," and he went in at the Victoria gate, with
Eve at his heels.

" Mister, how old might you be ? " she asked,
encouraged by the sound of his voice.

" Thirty."

" And you've passed ten years in—in there."
She jerked her head back and shivered a little.

He had stooped to pick up a leaf.   It was a
yellow leaf from a chestnut that reached into
the fog above them.   He picked it slowly to
pieces, drawing full draughts of air into his
lungs.   " Fifteen," he jerked out, " one time and
another.   'Cumulated, you know."   Pausing, he
added, in a matter-of-fact voice, " What I've
took would come to less 'n a pound's worth,
altogether."

The Gardens were deserted, and the pair
roamed towards the centre, gazing curiously at
so much of sodden vegetation as the fog allowed

them to see. Their eyes were not jaded; to them a blade of grass was not a little thing.

They were down on the south side, amid the heterogeneous plants there collected, examining each leaf, spelling the Latin labels and comparing them, when the hour came for closing. In the dense atmosphere the park-keeper missed them. The gates were shut; and the fog settled down thicker with the darkness.

Then the man and the woman were aware, and grew afraid. They saw only a limitless plain of grey about them, and heard a murmur as of the sea rolling around it.

"This gaol is too big," whispered Eve, and they took hands. The man trembled. Together they moved into the fog, seeking an outlet.

At the end of an hour or so they stumbled on a seat, and sat down for awhile to share the bread and sausage, and drink the gin. Eve was tired out and would have slept, but the man shook her by the shoulder.

"For God's sake don't leave me to face this alone. Can you sing?"

She began " *When other lips . . .* " in a whisper which gradually developed into a reedy soprano. She had forgotten half the words, but Adam lit a pipe and listened appreciatively.

" Tell you what," he said at the close ; " you'll be able to pick up a little on the road with your singing. We'll tramp west to-morrow, and pass ourselves off for man and wife. Likely we'll get some farm work, down in the country. Let's get out of this."

They joined hands and started off again, unable to see a foot before them in the blackness. So it happened next morning that the park-keeper, coming at his usual hour to unlock the gates, found a man and a woman inside with their white faces pressed against the railings, through which they glared like caged beasts. He set them free, and they ran out, for his paradise was too big.

Now, facing west, they tramped for two days on the Bath road, leaving the fog behind them, and drew near Reading. It was a clear night as they approached it, and the sky studded with

Q

stars that twinkled frostily. Eleven o'clock
sounded from a tower ahead. On the outskirts
of the town they were passing an ugly modern
villa with a large garden before it, when an old
gentleman came briskly up the road and turned
in at the gate.

Adam swung round on his heel and followed
him up the path, begging. Eve hung by the gate.

" No," said the old gentleman, fitting his
latchkey into the door, " I have no work to
offer. Eh ?—Is that your wife by the gate ?
Hungry ? "

Adam whispered a lie in his ear.

" Poor woman, and to be on the road, in
such a state, at this hour ! Well, you shall
share my supper before you search for a lodging.
Come inside," he called out to Eve, " and be
careful of the step. It's a high one."

He led them in, past the ground-floor rooms
and up a flight of stairs. After pausing on the
landing and waiting a long time for Eve to take
breath, he began to ascend another flight.

" Are we going to have supper on the
leads ? " Adam wondered.

They followed the old gentleman up to the attics and into a kind of tower, where was a small room with two tables spread, the one with a supper, the other with papers, charts, and mathematical instruments.

" Here," said their guide, " is bread, a cold chicken, and a bottle of whisky. I beg you to excuse me while you eat. The fact is, I dabble in astronomy. My telescope is on the roof above, and to-night every moment is precious."

There was a ladder fixed in the room, leading to a trap-door in the ceiling. Up this ladder the old gentleman trotted, and in half a minute had disappeared, shutting the trap behind him.

It was half an hour or more before Adam climbed after him, with Eve, as usual, at his heels.

" My dear madam ! " cried the astronomer, " and in your state ! "

" I told you a lie," Adam said. " I've come to beg your pardon. May we look at the stars before we go ? "

In two minutes the old gentleman was pointing out the constellations — the Great Bear

ϙ 2

hanging low in the north-east, pointing to the Pole star, and across it to Cassiopeia's bright zigzag high in the heavens; the barren square of Pegasus, with its long tail stretching to the Milky Way, and the points that cluster round Perseus; Arcturus, white Vega and yellow Capella; the Twins, and beyond them the Little Dog twinkling through a coppice of naked trees to eastward; yet further round the Pleiads climbing, with red Aldebaran after them; below them Orion's belt, and last of all, Sirius flashing like a diamond, white and red, and resting on the horizon where the dark pasture lands met the sky.

Then, growing flushed with his subject, he began to descant on these stars, their distances and velocities; how that each was a sun, careering in measureless space, each trailing a company of worlds that spun and hurtled round it; that the Dog-star's light shone into their eyes across a hundred trillion miles; that the star itself swept along a thousand miles in a minute. He hurled figures at them, heaping millions on millions. "See here"—and, turning the telescope on its pivot, he sighted it carefully.

"Look at that small star in the Great Bear: that's Groombridge Eighteen-thirty. *He's* two hundred billions of miles away. *He* travels two hundred miles a second, does Groombridge Eighteen-thirty. In one minute Groombridge Eighteen-thirty could go from here to Hong-Kong."

"Then damn Groombridge Eighteen-thirty !"

It was uttered in the bated tone that night enforces : but it came with a groan. The old gentleman faced round in amazement.

"He means, sir," explained the woman, who had grown to understand Adam passing well, " my man means that it's all too big for us. We've strayed out of prison, sir, and shall feel safer back again, looking at all this behind bars."

She reached out a hand to Adam : and this time it was he that followed, as one blinded and afraid. In three months they were back again at the gates of the paradise they had wandered from. There stood a warder before it, clad in blue : but he carried no flaming sword, and the door opened and let them in.

BESIDE THE BEE-HIVES.

On the outskirts of the village of Gantick stand two small semi-detached cottages, coloured with the same pale yellow wash, their front gardens descending to the high-road in parallel lines, their back gardens (which are somewhat longer) climbing to a little wood of secular elms, traditionally asserted to be the remnant of a mighty forest. The party hedge is heightened by a thick screen of white-thorn on which the buds were just showing pink when I took up my lodging in the left-hand cottage (the 10th of May by my diary); and at the end of it are two small arbours, set back to back, their dilapidated sides and roofs bound together by clematis.

The night of my arrival, my landlady asked me to make the least possible noise in unpacking my portmanteau, because there was trouble next door, and the partitions were thin. Our neighbour's wife was down with inflammation, she explained—inflammation of the lungs, as I learnt by a question or two. It was a bad case. She was a wisht, ailing soul to begin with. Also the owls in the wood above had been hooting loudly, for nights past: and yesterday a hedge-sparrow lit on the sill of the sick-room window, two sure tokens of approaching death. The sick woman was being nursed by her elder sister, who had lived in the house for two years, and practically taken charge of it. " Better the man had married *she*," my landlady added, somewhat unfeelingly.

I saw the man in his garden early next morning: a tall fellow, hardly yet on the wrong side of thirty, dressed in loose-fitting tweed coat and corduroys. A row of bee-hives stood along his side of the party wall, and he had taken the farthest one, which was empty, off its stand, and was rubbing it on the inside with a handful of elder-flower buds, by way of preparation for a new swarm. Even from my bed-room window I remarked, as he turned his head occasionally, that he was singularly handsome. His movements were those of a lazy man in a hurry, though there seemed no reason for hurry in his task. But when it was done, and the hive replaced, his behaviour began to be so eccentric that I paused in the midst of my shaving, to watch.

He passed slowly down the line of bee-hives, halting beside each in turn, and bending his head down close to the orifice with the exact action of a man whispering a secret into another's ear. I believe he kept this attitude for a couple of minutes beside each hive—there were eight, besides the empty one. At the end of the row he lifted his head, straightened his shoulders, and cast a glance up at my window, where I kept well out of sight. A minute after, he entered his house by the back door, and did not reappear.

At breakfast I asked my landlady if our neighbour were wrong in his head at all. She looked astonished, and answered, " No : he was a do-nothing fellow—unless you counted it hard work to drive a carrier's van thrice a week into Tregarrick, and home the same night. But he kept very steady, and had a name for good nature."

Next day the man was in his garden at the

same hour, and repeated the performance. Throughout the following night I was kept awake by a series of monotonous groans that reached me through the partition, and the murmur of voices speaking at intervals. It was horrible to lie within a few inches of the sick woman's head, to listen to her agony and be unable to help, unable even to see. Towards six in the morning, in bright daylight, I dropped off to sleep at last.

Two hours later the sound of voices came in at the open window and awoke me. I looked out into my neighbour's garden. He was standing, half-way up the path, in the sunshine, and engaged in a suppressed but furious altercation with a thin woman, some-what above middle height. Both wore thick green veils over their faces and thick gloves on their hands. The woman carried a rusty tea-tray.

The man stood against her, motioning her back towards the house. I caught a sentence— " It'll be the death of her;" and the woman glanced back over her shoulder towards the

window of the sick-room. She seemed about
to reply, but shrugged her shoulders instead
and went back into the house, carrying her tray.
The man turned on his heel, walked hurriedly
up the garden, and scrambled over its hedge
into the wood. His veil and thick gloves were
explained a couple of hours later, when I looked
into the garden again and saw him hiving a
swarm of bees that he had captured, the first
of the season.

That same afternoon, about four o'clock, I
observed that every window in the next house
stood wide open. My landlady was out in the
garden, " picking in" her week's washing from
the thorn hedge where it had been suspended
to dry; and I called her attention to this new
freak of our neighbours.

" Ah, then, the poor soul must be nigh to
her end," said she. " That's done to give her
an easy death."

The woman died at half-past seven. And
next morning her husband hung a scrap of
black crape to each of the bee-hives.

She was buried on Sunday afternoon. From

behind the drawn blinds of my sitting-room window I saw the funeral leave the house and move down the front garden to the high-road —the heads of the mourners, each with a white handkerchief pressed to its nose, appearing above the wall like the top of a procession in some Assyrian sculpture. The husband wore a ridiculously tall hat, and a hat-band with long tails. The whole affair had the appearance of an hysterical outrage on the afternoon sunshine. At the foot of the garden they struck up a "burying tune," and passed down the road, shouting it with all their lungs.

I caught up a book and rushed out into the back garden for fresh air. Even out of doors it was insufferably hot, and soon I flung myself down on the bench within the arbour and set myself to read. A plank behind me had started, and after a while the edge of it began to gall my shoulders as I leant back. I tried once or twice to push it into its place, without success, and then, in a moment of irritation, gave it a tug. It came away in my hand, and something rolled out on the bench before me, and broke in two.

I picked it up. It was a lump of dough, rudely moulded to the shape of a woman, with a rusty brass-headed nail stuck through the breast. Around the body was tied a lock of fine light-brown hair—a woman's, by its length.

After a careful examination, I untied the lock of hair, put the doll back in its place behind the plank, and returned to the house: for I had a question or two to put to my landlady.

"Was the dead woman at all like her elder sister?" I asked. "Was she black-haired, for instance?"

"No," answered my landlady; "she was shorter and much fairer. You might almost call her a light-haired woman."

I hoped she would pardon me for changing the subject abruptly and asking an apparently ridiculous question, but would she call a man mad if she found him whispering secrets into a bee-hive?

My landlady promptly replied that, on the contrary, she would think him extremely sensible; for that, unless bees were told of all that was happening in the household to which they belonged, they might consider themselves neglected, and leave the place in wrath. She asserted this to be a notorious fact.

"I have one more question," I said. "Suppose that you found in your garden a lock of hair—a lock such as this, for instance—what would you do with it?"

She looked at it, and caught her breath sharply.

"I'm no meddler," she said at last; "I should burn it."

"Why?"

"Because if 'twas left about, the birds might use it for their nests, and weave it in so tight that the owner couldn't rise on Judgment day."

So I burnt the lock of hair in her presence; because I wanted its owner to rise on Judgment day and state a case which, after all, was no affair of mine.

THE MAGIC SHADOW.

ONCE upon a time there was born a man-child with a magic shadow.

His case was so rare that a number of doctors have been disputing over it ever since and picking his parents' histories and genealogies to bits, to find the cause. Their inquiries do not help us much. The father drove a cab; the mother was a charwoman and came of a consumptive family. But these facts will not quite account for a magic shadow. The birth took place on the night of a new moon, down a narrow alley into which neither moon nor sun ever penetrated beyond the third-storey windows —and that is why the parents were so long in discovering their child's miraculous gift. The hospital-student who attended merely remarked that the babe was small and sickly, and advised the mother to drink sound port-wine while nursing him,—which she could not afford.

Nevertheless, the boy struggled somehow

through five years of life, and was put into small-
clothes. Two weeks after this promotion his
mother started off to scrub out a big house in
the fashionable quarter, and took him with her :
for the house possessed a wide garden, laid with
turf and lined with espaliers, sunflowers, and
hollyhocks, and as the month was August, and
the family away in Scotland, there seemed no
harm in letting the child run about in this
paradise while she worked. A flight of steps
descended from the drawing-room to the garden,
and as she knelt on her mat in the cool room
it was easy to keep an eye on him. Now
and then she gazed out into the sunshine and
called; and the boy stopped running about and
nodded back, or shouted the report of some
fresh discovery.

By-and-by a sulphur butterfly excited him
so that he must run up the broad stone steps
with the news. The woman laughed, looking at
his flushed face, then down at his shoe-strings,
which were untied : and then she jumped up,
crying out sharply—"Stand still, child—stand
still a moment!"

She might well stare. Her boy stood and smiled in the sun, and his shadow lay on the whitened steps. Only the silhouette was not that of a little breeched boy at all, but of a little girl in petticoats ; and it wore long curls, whereas the charwoman's son was close-cropped.

The woman stepped out on the terrace to look closer. She twirled her son round and walked him down into the garden, and backwards and forwards, and stood him in all manner of positions and attitudes, and rubbed her eyes. But there was no mistake : the shadow was that of a little girl.

She hurried over her charing, and took the boy home for his father to see before sunset. As the matter seemed important, and she did not wish people in the street to notice anything strange, they rode back in an omnibus. They might have spared their haste, however, as the cab-driver did not reach home till supper-time, and then it was found that in the light of a candle, even when stuck inside a carriage-lamp, their son cast just an ordinary shadow. But next morning at sunrise they woke him up and

R

carried him to the house-top, where the sunlight slanted between the chimney-stacks: and the shadow was that of a little girl.

The father scratched his head. "There's money in this, wife. We'll keep the thing close; and in a year or two he'll be fit to go round in a show and earn money to support our declining years."

With that the poor little one's misfortunes began. For they shut him in his room, nor allowed him to play with the other children in the alley—there was no knowing what harm might come to his precious shadow. On dark nights his father walked him out along the streets; and the boy saw many curious things under the gas-lamps, but never the little girl who inhabited his shadow. So that by degrees he forgot all about her. And his father kept silence.

Yet all the while she grew side by side with him, keeping pace with his years. And on his fifteenth birthday, when his parents took him out into the country and, in the sunshine there, revealed his secret, she was indeed a companion to be proud of—neat of figure, trim of ankle, with masses of waving hair; but whether blonde or brunette could not be told; and, alas! she had no eyes to look into.

"My son," said they, "the world lies before you. Only do not forget your parents, who conferred on you this remarkable shadow."

The youth promised, and went off to a showman. The showman gladly hired him; for, of course, a magic shadow was a rarity, though not so well paying as the Strong Man or the Fat Woman, for these were worth seeing every day, whereas for weeks at a time, in dull weather or foggy, our hero had no shadow at all. But he earned enough to keep himself and help the parents at home; and was considered a success.

One day, after five years of this, he sought the Strong Man, and sighed. For they had become close friends.

"I am in love," he confessed.

"With your shadow?"

"No."

"Not with the Fat Woman!" the Strong Man exclaimed, with a start of jealousy.

"No. I have seen her that I mean these three days in the Square, on her way to music lesson. She has dark brown eyes and wears yellow ribbons. I love her."

"You don't say so! She has never come to our performance, I hope."

"It has been foggy ever since we came to this town."

"Ah, to be sure. Then there's a chance: for, you see, she would never look at you if she knew of—of that other. Take my advice—go into society, always at night, when there is no danger;-get introduced; dance with her; sing serenades under her window; then marry her. Afterwards—well, that's your affair."

So the youth went into society and met the girl he loved, and danced with her so vivaciously and sang serenades with such feeling beneath her window, that at last she felt he was all in all to her. Then the youth asked to be allowed to see her father, who was a Retired Colonel; and professed himself a man of Substance. He said nothing of the Shadow : but it is true he had saved a certain amount. " Then to all intents and purposes you are a gentle-man," said the Retired Colonel ; and the wed-ding-day was fixed.

They were married in dull weather, and spent a delightful honeymoon. But when spring came and brighter days, the young wife began to feel lonely ; for her husband locked himself, all the day long, in his study—to work, as he said. He seemed to be always at work ; and whenever he consented to a holiday, it was sure to fall on the bleakest and dismallest day in the week.

" You are never so gay now as you were last Autumn. I am jealous of that work of yours. At least," she pleaded, " let me sit with you and share your affection with it."

But he laughed and denied her : and next day she peered in through the keyhole of his study.

That same evening she ran away from him : having seen the shadow of another woman by his side.

Then the poor man—for he had loved his

wife—cursed the day of his birth and led an evil life. This lasted for ten years, and his wife died in her father's house, unforgiving.

On the day of her funeral, the man said to his shadow—" I see it all. We were made for each other, so let us marry. You have wrecked my life and now must save it. Only it is rather hard to marry a wife whom one can only see by sunlight and moonlight."

So they were married; and spent all their life in the open air, looking on the naked world and learning its secrets. And his shadow bore him children, in stony ways and on the bare mountain-side. And for every child that was born the man felt the pangs of it.

And at last he died and was judged: and being interrogated concerning his good deeds, began—

" We two——"

—and looked around for his shadow. A great light shone all about; but she was nowhere to be seen. In fact, she had passed before him; and his children remained on earth, where men already were heaping them with flowers and calling them divine.

Then the man folded his arms and lifted his chin.

"I beg your pardon," he said, "I am simply a sinner."

There are in this world certain men who create. The children of such are poems, and the half of their soul is female. For it is written that without woman no new thing shall come into the world.

THE END.